William Sharp

Wives in Exile

A Comedy in Romance

William Sharp

Wives in Exile
A Comedy in Romance

ISBN/EAN: 9783744779968

Printed in Europe, USA, Canada, Australia, Japan

Cover: Foto ©Andreas Hilbeck / pixelio.de

More available books at **www.hansebooks.com**

WIVES IN EXILE

A Comedy in Romance

BY

WILLIAM SHARP

LAMSON, WOLFFE AND COMPANY

BOSTON, NEW YORK AND LONDON

MDCCCXCVI

𝔘niversity 𝔓ress
John Wilson & Son, Cambridge, U.S.A.

" No woman had done it yet."

The Amazing Marriage.

WIVES IN EXILE

CHAPTER I.

" THERE are many who know how to write ; there are few who know how to live."

"My dearest Honor, is that wise saying yours, or Wilfrid's, or — or — the Reverend James's?"

"James, my dear Leonora, would not say it if he believed it. He is a man in whom knowledge is native."

" Knowledge of what? "

"Of his own omniscience."

" And then? "

" Why, then, he is of that class of persons who know so much that they don't know the — the — what shall I say — the simplest of insuperable difficulties ; how to live."

I   I

In the bright room there was a sound of comfort. It may have come from the fire of sea-coal that burned with flashes of blue and guinea-yellow flame, or from the spurtive hissing of a silver tea-urn that, surrounded by small basins, jugs, and cups and saucers, seemed like some fantastic ship out of Cathay girt by ludicrous small craft. Or it may have arisen from the nocturnal gloom and wet without, in contrast with the quietude and opulent light and warmth within. The rain no longer lashed horizontally, but dribbled and drizzled with an incoherent murmur against the panes. The unspent gale, however, rose and fell with strange persistency. It had the moan of the sea in its dreary sough, as in the wet pine-tree in the garden we may hear the singular cry of the hill-wind. When it came round the eastern gable of the Royal Erin Hotel it had a peculiar note of desolation. The fell iniquity of its perversity, as Mrs. Adair, parodying Sir Thomas Browne, described it, was, she added, as maladroit an occurrence as though it were the fulfilment of a set purpose on the part of a male providence.

Within, the insolent glare of the gas betrayed the radical unheed of the Royal Erin Hotel to any intemperance of the weather. The room was not, perhaps, a delight to the eyes of sensitive persons. There was so vast an expanse of white, with curtains and couches and chairs and spindle-legged lounges in a scarlet so blatant that it suggested the blood of martyrs, shed here with unstinted if judiciously regulated prodigality. The crystal chandelier was suspended by a brazen abomination, wrought with unspeakable disregard for common seemliness even. Tattered muslin fly-guards hung limply upon three of its five branches. The effect was that of Medusa's head in curls; a Medusa who had seen better days. On the blank north wall of white and gold paper hung a large colored print of the baptismal ceremony of Queen Victoria's first-born. On the blank south wall were two oleographs; the conflict of the *Shannon* and the *Chesapeake*, and Prince Albert assisting his royal spouse to dismount from a shaggy pony that had come to a halt in a pre-eminently picturesque Highland glen. The east and west walls

3

were better. Midway in the latter was the door, oaken to the eye, if polishable deal to the contractor. To the left of it was a mirror, round which a cloud of pink gauze was tufted in exactly regular clumps. It was the most delightful thing in the room, for it reflected the bright hearth and ruddy flames opposite, two large armchairs covered with white dimity, and in these chairs Mrs. Leonora Wester and Mrs. Honor Adair.

To have a bright fire and an adjacent mirror; that, certainly, is to have opened at least the first seal of enjoyment. The second is already broken when one can look into the mirror and see oneself at one's best, touched with that remote grace which is so seductively obvious in pools and shallows and mirrors, and so apt to prove evasive in the hand-glass. Yet another seal is broken when we can view, beside Ideala, the form and features, and answering eyes of one who is as blithe to the mind as she, or he, is dear to the heart.

This third seal was denied to Mrs. Adair. From her position she could obtain no more than a glimpse of the escritoire, that stood beyond her friend and the fireplace, and of the burnished copper-gold hair that was pressed against the ridge of the arm-chair. Mrs. Wester was more fortunate. She enjoyed the vision of her own fair beauty and the dark loveliness of Honor Adair. The contrast was admirable. She delighted in it with an impersonal joy. She, as she saw herself, was so wrought of white and gold that she was an August morning, where wind and sunshine have taken possession of the dew-wet wheat. Her eyes were of that deep blue which in emotion becomes violet. The white clove she wore at her breast seemed as though it had fallen from the brown and gold tangle of her hair, which was all of waving lines and sudden rebellious sprays. So cream white was her complexion that her lips would have gleamed too redly but that they were so delicate in form and of so dainty a curve. Looking from herself to her companion she noted how dark was the beautiful hair that clustered around Honor's head, — set upon a high neck with a poise as of a sea-wave ; it too had lines of gold in it, as though a sun-ray had been meshed therein

5

and never yet escaped, if escape it would. Yes, she admitted, Honor was the more lovely, at least to her taste. If she were a man, she would fall in love with this tall beautiful creature that was at once so self-possessed a young woman and of so wild a nature that a word could lure her to the maddest fantasy, or affright with remote silences beyond ordinary dumbness. How glad she was that both were tall. Men of a romantic temperament prefer tall women, she remembered to have heard.

"Honor," she asked abruptly at this juncture, "would you say that he is of a romantic temperament?"

"My dear Nora, do not tantalize me with a riddle that promises to resolve itself so delightfully. Be plain with me if you value my peace of mind — or yours. Who is *HE* ?"

"Why, Richard, my husband, of course."

Mrs. Adair looked at her friend with a curious expression. That "*of course*" opened appalling perspectives of marital felicity. Mrs. Adair was not sentimental. She always declared she was not cynical. She was certainly in love with Wilfrid Adair. But, after three years, to allude to a romantic "*He*," or a "*He*" in connection with romantic sentiment, and to wed this "*He*" to an "of course" of relativity to one's husband, this, indeed, was strange. She knew Leonora. She knew Richard Parkins Wester. They were happy; they were well content; they were well suited, the one to the other. But Mr. Wester was not the likeliest person to identify with a "He" of romance. Honor Adair had come to Dublin to embark on a somewhat novel voyage. A minute ago she had thrilled to the exciting thought that she was on the verge of a not less alluring mental excursion. It was disappointing to be arrested at the last moment by so insignificant a familiarity as Mr. Wester.

"Oh, Richard, your husband, — of course."

"Honor, you absurd girl, what is voyaging through that mysterious mind of yours?"

"Nothing. I was dreaming. The rain and the wind charm one into happy silences as much as — as much as — the conversation of a person of a romantic temperament!"

" *Conversation* — no ! That would be flying in the face of Providence. The sweetest conversation *à deux* is when it is all on one side and in a low voice. We might even go so far as to say a whisper. But come ! You have not answered my question."

" Your question ? — Oh, yes, of course, I remember. Well, — "

" Oh, never mind. It does not matter now. I too was thinking of some one else — some one whom you do not know."

" Tell me."

" What ? "

" About the some one."

" Do not be absurd. No ; I tell you frankly myself that I do not think Richard exactly romantic. He maintains he is. He bases this belief on the fact that it was on a Friday he asked me to marry him, and, that, moreover, married we were on a Friday."

" Well, that's about as much romance as one can fairly look for in marriage."

" Now, Honor, you know you are riding your tongue with a spur, as they say."

" Wilfrid and I had a much more romantic experience. The tide went out, however, all

8

the same. The tide seems always to be on the ebb immediately after it reaches the altar. We, too, were married on a Friday; but while your Friday was a nondescript fifth day (I never knew whether it should be called fifth or sixth) ours was the 31st of October, — Hallowmas Eve. To be married on the day of Hallowe'en is to play at skittles with an offended deity, the wedded couple being the skittles of course. But to be married at Hallowtide when it happens to fall on a Friday is to invite Satan to your house as an honored guest, and then needlessly insult him by a gift of the Shorter Catechism or an S. P. C. K. pamphlet."

"But did it make *no* difference to you and Wilfrid?"

"Certainly. It amused us. It annoyed his people."

"But in the matter of romance?"

"In the matter of romance I must admit that it did not have much effect."

"Did it not draw you closer?"

"Why should it?"

"Oh — well — the knowledge that you had done something that made people shiver with

9

apprehension, or frown, or put on a Sabbath-morning aspect of all uncharitableness."

"Did you and Richard draw closer on account of *your* Friday transgression?"

"No, I can't say we did. We quarrelled about it."

"Ah."

"I hated the idea. It seemed so wanton a tempting of — *something.*"

"Why did you do it, then?"

"I did not know till after we were married: I mean, I never thought about it. The very first thing that, as Mrs. Wester, I asked Richard to do for me, he refused. I requested him to forget that his heedless parent had given him Parkins as a second name; and in any case to cease from allusion to, or even from signing as, Richard P. He refused. I told him he had no imagination; if he had, he would have known that a sensitive woman could not be quite happy with such an initial as P. sandwiched into her married designation. What could one expect of an unextended P. but that it heralded Peter, or Potts, or Prodgers, or some other horror?

"Richard said it might just as likely be Plantagenet, or Percy, or Penrhyn. 'Oh,' I went on, 'you might adduce Pericles or Pindar or anything you like from Plato to Periwinkle, — *only it did not alter the case.*' Richard looked bewildered. '*What case?*' he asked, with that maddening thirst for the hard fact which is so intolerable in a man when he is no longer an anxious lover. I begged him to think for a moment. I was certain to have quite sufficiently a hard time of it, in Brooklyn and New York, among married and unmarried women *there*, without having to hang out a signboard as to a tender spot being ready to hand. *Of course*, they would fasten on that wretched P. 'Why in Heaven's name should they?' he demanded with absurd warmth : 'more men in America went through life with a second name contracted to an initial than the census could tackle.' He said it was more difficult to slough than a bad reputation. I said it *was* a bad reputation, — to go about with an unexplained P., *in Society.*"

"What did he say to that, Leonora?"

"Richard is concise. He said: 'Damn Society.'"

"And he nailed P. to the mast, and said that he would sink rather than surrender."

"No such luck. When a man says he will never surrender he proves what identical animals men and women are."

"Women always surrender, you think?"

"No. But they always do when they swear they won't. No man — I don't mean a male creature, but a man — would dream of relinquishing his desire of a woman because she told him she would never surrender."

"Because in the very saying so she would have already opened the outer gates."

"Exactly. Well, to return to Richard. He repeated his remark. '*Yes: damn it.*' These were his exact words. 'It is easy to damn life in the moon,' I said. 'Oh, come now, Leonora,' he replied: 'New York State isn't Kamtchatka, and I *have* moved about a bit in Mayfair.'

"'A man may travel in strange company,' was my response: 'but no woman who respects herself can afford to go about with an indefinite P.' 'Oh, this is too absurd,' exclaimed my husband; 'for the sake of our future happiness let us unchain P. and send him forth conquering and to conquer us Parkins.'"

"Nora, *ma chérie*, what has all this to do with imagination, and your Friday quarrel?"

"I was just coming to it. I flatly told him, that rather than be known as Mrs. Parkins Wester I would part from him there and then. I complained that he had no imagination. He said he had. He then informed me as to his recklessness about both proposing and marrying on a Friday. Of course I was able triumphantly to maintain that our quarrel was due to that wanton flying in the face of common prejudice. 'How about the outcome of the first Friday,' he demanded. However, I left him in high chagrin, and we did not speak again till shortly before dinner."

"And Mr. Wester retained P.?"

"Yes, but with a compromise. He said he would tell no one what it stood for: what was more to the point, he added that he would hint it was a mysterious designation, —

the name of a country, to suggest intimate relationships of a peculiar kind. 'There are only Palestine and Peru,' I objected; 'the first suggests Jewish extraction, and the second an agency in nitrate.' 'There is Persia,' he said quietly. I saw the light through *that* chink. Except some detestable Parkinses who live in Massachusetts, and a few irresponsible persons in New York, no one knows that Parkins holds on with a despairing clutch to 'Wester.' We have had a lot of fun out of 'Persia.' Only the other day, at Mountmichael, when that awful creature Mr. Stapleton Fogo asked if my husband were any relation of some R. Pringle Wester in London, I said, with an air of condescension: 'I thought every one knew that Mr. Wester was called after the ancient and royal country of Persia, where — but no, state-secrets were state-secrets!' You should have seen the Reverend James's face. He drew me aside afterwards, and remonstrated. 'Have I been mistaken, my dear Leonora,' he asked, 'in taking Mr. Wester's second name to be, not *Persia*, but *Parkins ?*' 'My dearest James,' I replied, 'as the Rev. Lord Curraghmore, you are too amusing for anything.' — ' But a fact, Leonora, is a fact.' — ' Rarely, my dear James!' — 'A fact not a fact! Why —' But here I interjected a remark : ' Go, my dear brother : you do not understand women. A wrinkle, a gray hair, a rheumatic twinge, each of these is a fact. A name is not a fact. A ranunculus is not a ranunculus (which is nothing at all), but only a flower that for convenience' sake we call a ranunculus. If Persia suits us better than Parkins there is no commandment to break in our adoption of it, save that against fibbing ; but what is a stray fib in the universal hurly-burly of things? Now go, I say ; go and rejoin Stapleton Fogo, and tell him, if you like, that I had a sunstroke in Persia, and have had an affection for the name ever since. And then fetch me a cup of tea, and for Heaven's sake don't look so serious!' "

Mrs. Adair sat back in her lounge-chair and laughed that low music of hers which set men's hearts a-beating.

"You are too delightful, Leonora. I suppose you are even now talking wildly at random."

"At random, my dear Honor? Never was I more serious. Hark to that wind! Think upon what we have put our hands to do!"

"It is what we have been thinking of all the time we have been speaking."

"Alas, yes."

"I wonder if Harry has managed everything rightly at Queenstown."

"We ought to have heard from him. Wretch that he is to keep two beautiful women hanging upon a word from his lips. Oh, Honor, let us make him pay for it some day."

"He is married, alas."

"So much the easier for us. A man rolls off his little hill so easily when he thinks he has settled himself at the summit like a boulder."

"But then" —

"Yes, to be sure. But now let us leave Harry Adair in the mean time. I wonder what Wilfrid and Mr. Wester are doing in London at this moment."

"They will be at a theatre, or at a club — perhaps discussing us. Woman is an endless theme for men."

"*Women,* my dear Nora. There is a distinction. Women are interested in woman, men in women."

"If they *are* discussing us, I hope their consciences smite them."

"The male conscience follows the example of its intimate friend, the liver. It is apt to get sluggish early in life. No, *camerado mio,* if our husbands are discussing women, it is not likely we are in it, — save as menacing shadows in the background!"

"Do you think men *never* think about their wives when they are away from them?"

"Of course they think about them. They have always 'a lot of things to remember.' But after a year or so of marriage they bear up. It is wonderful how patient in endurance a married man can be, separated from his wife."

"Could you be jealous, Honor? I was going to say, are you jealous? But I don't believe so beautiful a woman as yourself could possibly have cause."

"How sweet of you, Nora. As to jealousy, — well, I don't know. I am not of a jealous temperament, so far as that goes. They say that women are always more jealous than men. I don't believe it. They are more exacting in little things, I grant. A jealous woman, too, commits a greater mistake than a jealous man does, — and to commit a mistake is, as you know, more often fatal than to break several commandments. Be jealous, and your husband will be disloyal to you in word and deed; do not be jealous, and he will at any rate be open with you orally. For a woman, particularly for a wife, to exhibit jealousy, is to close a promising well-spring of interest. It is as though one were to go to the theatre to hear a comedy, but to stop up one's ears beforehand. A man will dissect his reputation to a sympathetic wife, and enjoy the experience. A shade of jealousy — and the gay Jack of the past is buried as a Sadducee in the sedate John of respectability."

"That is all very well of certain men. The majority of the species is uninteresting."

"Of course."

18

"Who would care to have the confidences of the respectable Johns? Most of them have enjoyed a flirtation with a barmaid, glorify it with an imaginary aureole, and allude to it as an early romance. Besides, — to the elect of the earth there are only a few men and women who are really interesting. The vast majority of persons consists merely of tedious tracts with an obvious moral. The others are more or less clever and interesting novels. Now and again we encounter a romance."

"The worst of encountering a 'romance' is that we are so apt to fall in love with 'him' or 'her.'"

"Don't you think a good deal depends in the attitude of the 'romance'? It is certainly apt to be irresistible if it make the first move. I grant that. But its appearance is so rare that we are as likely as not to set ourselves to enjoy it spectacularly, as a blasé theatre-goer suddenly finds himself witnessing something at once really novel and striking and superbly acted."

"I wonder if romance — I mean the real thing — is the paramount prerogative of either sex. I mean, are women in the main, or are men in the main, more romantic? What do you think, Leonora?"

"I think the difference is that of incident and episode. Romance lies more in incident for men, on the whole, I think. In episode, which does not necessarily involve peril or any hazard for the body, but is much more an occasion for the adventurous or curious spirit, women range more freely and naturally than men. A *real* episode is always a tragi-comedy for a woman, even when the sun shines throughout and all ends well. For a man it is a glorified incident. Of course, there are men — and men. A manly man, of the finest breed, is one third woman. Other men can lead romantic lives, can have romantic experiences; it is only men of this rare kind who are in themselves romantic."

"Well, my dear, that brings us round to your question: Do I think Richard Wester romantic? I have already given you my answer."

"How cruel even a friend can be. However, I forgive you. I brought it upon myself. And now, dear, I must go and write my letter for to-morrow's American mail. What shall you do? Have you a book? Ah, here is a good idea. We said we would collaborate in a novel some day. Let us begin now. Here we are on the verge of an unconventional experience. It ought to stimulate us. Come, Honor, you make the first plunge while I am writing my long letter. Let it be anything you like, — a novel, a short story, a fantasy, an essay! I am ready to accommodate you, you see!"

"Nonsense, Nora. You know that neither of us can write. It was an absurd idea. No; I have my journal here, if I want to occupy myself. I prefer looking into the fire and dreaming. Besides, after all, the last post may not be here yet. There is still time to hear from Harry Adair. If he does n't write he 's sure to telegraph. You go and write your letter. If I feel inclined I 'll commit my valuable memoranda to my diary."

"Oh, are you not excited? *I* am. How good it is to be alive! But do, do let us write something together some day. What if writing be supremely difficult for one, and almost impossible *à deux!* Honestly, I would rather know how to write than anything else. I — "

" There are many who know how to write: there are few who know how to live."

The words that followed are already on record.

Mrs. Wester had not yet risen from her chair in front of the fire, and from her surreptitious contemplation of herself and Mrs. Adair in the opposite mirror, when a waiter entered bearing a small salver on which was the brown envelope of a telegram.

Leonora shredded the cover with avidity. She scanned it with the eagerness of a windhover over a young partridge-brood. Having dismissed the waiter, she read the message to her companion. Her voice had in it the tragi-comedy of 'a real (feminine) episode.' The telegram ran thus : —

To Mrs. Leonora Wester,
Royal Erin Hotel, Dublin.

The *Belle Aurore* sailed early this morning. Delay due to difficulty in obtaining scratch male crew for the occasion. Your own crew declined to sail on account of the weather. They go north by rail to-night. Mrs. Moriarty or Miss Macfee will call in the early morning for final instructions. Have written.

H. ADAIR.

CHAPTER II.

"AND now, my dear Jocelyn, I must tell you about *my* doings." So began the second part of Mrs. Wester's letter to her friend in Brooklyn, Mrs. Rivers.

Leonora was now the sole occupant of the drawing-room in the Royal Erin Hotel. She had deserted the arm-chair, the fire, and the mirror, for the escritoire, where, before beginning her letter to Mrs. Rivers, she had sat for some time meditating a missive to Mr. Wester.

"Yes: Honor is right," she muttered, as she slowly tore up the two sheets whereon appeared nothing further than, on the one, "Dearest Richard," and on the other, "My dear Richard." "Assuredly, as she says, it will be time enough to write to our husbands when once we have started. There's many a slip, &c.: and since that annoying and ridiculous telegram from Harry I feel as

24

though the Fates were against us, — worse than that, as if they were laughing at us. No : I 'll write to Jocelyn, and then go to bed. Now that I think of it, there is nothing out of the common in these creatures having refused to sail in the *Belle Aurore*, not because the weather was so bad, but because yesterday was Friday. How stupid of me to forget. Of course that is it. I have often heard that sailors hate to sail on a Friday. I wonder if I should go and tell Honor about this? Oh no, it will do when I go upstairs."

A sigh of relief, and she drew some note-paper towards her. With the rapidity natural to one who could lounge with such complete indolence and grace, she drove her pen along the white pages, response after response to Mrs. Rivers' remarks and questions charging swiftly as a battalion of horse. Erelong Part I. ended with an italicised *And now !*

" How it would delight you, dear Jocelyn, to be here just now, — that is, to be here with us, at this moment, on our present venture. We are playing off our own bat : *comprenez vous, ma chére ?*

"Who are 'we,' you will say — for, married dame as you are, you will at once have jumped to the conclusion that my allusion is not to Richard and myself. You have heard me speak of her, — I mean the other part of 'we.' For a 'her' (should I say a 'she') it (she) is. Honor Adair is too delightful for anything. Not only is she beautiful (come now, Jocelyn, don't smile, and for my part I 'll be frank) — as beautiful a brunette as I am a blonde, only I honestly think much more so : but she is also as blithe and brave and independent and altogether sweet and dear a girl as ever you saw, or are like to see. She is taller than I am, though I am fairly tall as you know. Let me see ; you cannot have forgotten about her? When Richard came over to Ireland three years ago it was, you may remember, to visit his Oxford friend Wilfrid Adair. It was while at Adair's place, Martin's Hope, that he met and chummed with 'the late Lord Curraghmore,' as he always alluded to my father. He took an equally immediate and pronounced dislike to my brother, 'The Reverend James,' as we invariably call the present Lord Curraghmore. When he was making up his mind to lay his heart and fortune at my feet (strange that *since* marriage his fortune has, in rising from my feet to my hands, dwindled extraordinarily in the process!) I was under the impression that the object of his affections, — a conventional phrase singularly in keeping with the men we know and meet, whatever of consuming passion the men of fiction may have, — was no other than Honor O'Connell, the daughter of that Terence O'Connell, Squire of Tansor, who a year before had been killed in the hunting field. Honor was at the time staying with her maternal uncle, Dr. Septimus Malone, who had a pretty little place wedged in between Mountmichael and Martin's Hope. By the way, did you know that Wilfrid Adair is my cousin? However the upshot was that I became Mrs. Richard Parkins Wester and Honor a few months later changed her name from O'Connell to Adair. As a matter of fact we had all four fallen in love, and become engaged, about the same time. Cousin though he was, I had never seen much of Wilfrid. He was, in my time

(dear me, what an atrocious phrase, sugges-
tive of matronly stoutness, whist parties, and
premature piety), an absentee landlord, and
marriage has n't much improved him in this
respect.   Honor is too pretty to wish to bury
herself in the country.   She is too innocent,
the dear thing !   She loves the country (and
truly I believe), and does not imagine that
the implied homage she meets with in London every time she stirs from the door is a
very tolerable incense indeed.   She would,
no doubt, love the country longer than her
husband, if she had to put up with both con-
tinuously and unmodified.   The country can
become a minister of apathy, but a husband
(in the country) can be as bitters without
the fit concomitant.   A pretty woman like
Honor is so delightfully self-sophisticated.
She believes she can thrive without the company of her fellows, particularly her fellow-
women.   As a matter of fact, she would be
more independent than most women for, say
a week ; perhaps two ; possibly three.   Then
the woman in her would mutiny.   That 's
when and where the peril comes in.   If a
woman like Honor yields then, — sensibly

caves in — well, all 's well that ends well.
If she does n't, there 's an imitation French
Revolution brewing ; or a volcanic eruption ;
or, at the very least, what Richard concisely
calls ' ructions.' I daresay Wilfrid Adair —
who adores her — sees the polish off the
mahogany occasionally, to quote Richard
again. I have never seen her in a rage, but
I 've had glimpses of her hanging around the
crates. Richard says she has a devil of a
controlled temper. He is often very vague
in his epithets. I know what you are saying
or thinking, my dear Jocelyn : O that this
Mrs. Adair had the equable sweetness and
suavity of my dearest Leonora !

"Dear me, how I am wandering. You
want to know, of course, how, when, and
why we — Honor and I — are about to play
off our bat.

"You will have received ere this my brief
note from Mountmichael, — or did I write
from Queenstown ? At any rate when Richard and I reached my brother's place we
found Wilfrid and Honor Adair to be guests
like ourselves of the Reverend James. Wilfrid had let Martin's Hope, and had accepted

Lord Curraghmore's invitation to spend a few weeks at Mountmichael while Mr. and Mrs. Wester were there.

"'Je serai bref, car j'aspire à des conclusions immédiates,' says Sainte Beuve, in a volume of his essays which I was reading on the Sunday of our voyage ; and I cannot do better than try to follow his example, — or rather his precept, the wretch, for I think he rambles frightfully. I wonder whether men or women are most discursive. I must say I think men are less concise (except when they are giving expression to their temper), less direct. What a pity some one does not invent a man-microscope ! What a delight it would be to look into the minds and souls and actual lives of men, — I mean of men who interest us. Even one's husband would be profoundly interesting. Honor admits she does not wholly know Wilfrid, and *perhaps* there are certain shallows in Richard's nature which I have not examined, or rather discovered. Think what — but no, I *will* keep to the point.

"Where were we? Oh, yes, at Mountmichael. Let me admit straightway that we all four — after the first few days — began to weary.   We found the local society dull, and the Reverend James duller.   The summer has been a glorious one, but the prolonged heat has got into the blood, and man, woman, and child yearn for a move into a cooler air.

" The bolt fell thus.

" I was in the hammock in the pine-grove which abuts on the tennis-ground.   I had fallen asleep.   Aroused by voices, I was soon aware that my husband at any rate was present.   No man ever had such a chuckle, as I 've often told him.

" What 's up, old chap?' I heard some one — Wilfrid — ask.

" 'Wilfrid Adair, have you read Montaigne?'

" I was amazed.   Richard is not literary in his taste for reading, though, as he says, he is fond of books that will either soothe him as an opium-draught or rouse him as a hurricane.

" Wilfrid said he had, and added that the copy in Richard's hands was his wife's, given her by Lord Curraghmore as a birthday-present, and with an accompanying warning.

"'He lives on the branch, does Master Montaigne. What do you think of this in general: "*As soon as women are ours, we are no longer theirs;*" and — and now, Wilfrid Adair, you mark me well — of this *in particular:* "*The yoke of love is sometimes heavier than that of all the virtues.*"'

"That wretch, Wilfrid, answered, with a sigh, — positively with a sigh, and added: 'Yes, my dear fellow, the tyranny of love demands more than a nation in despair could venture to ask.'

"I was now determined to listen. I had just been about to go away, or to make my neighborhood known.

"'Have n't seen any of those yokes loose about Mountmichael, have you?' asked my husband, with that graceless lack of good feeling and proper English to which I have drawn his attention again and again.

"I know what you mean, old man. But what are we to do. I admit that another month here will be apt to produce confirmed melancholia. But Curraghmore 's such a touchy chap.'

"'His sister, you know, has something of

his nature.' This was uttered by Richard in as cold and passionless a voice as though he were asking for a match, only with less real interest.

"I wonder they did not hear my gasp. Mr. Wester's injustice and callousness maddened me. I tell *you* of it, dear Jocelyn, to let you see what even an adored wife has to put up with from a husband. Don't tell *me* 'that a man's a man whate'er betide.' A married man is a thing by itself; a distinct genus.

"There was a silence after this of at least five minutes. I heard their outgiven breath as they smoked. Strange that men should require to ruminate so long. They would not care to be likened to cows. Why then do they so provokingly invite the comparison?

"At last Richard spoke.

"'Adair, my boy!'

"'Well?'

"'In three months time I must be back in New York. If one gives two thirds of one's time to one's wife in a long holiday one does the square thing, don't you think so? Just so: I thought you would. Now I propose that you and I accept Gustav Andersen's invitation that he made us in Norway. Thence we can go to Scotland, and have some shooting at your cousin's place.'

" ' Good; so far as Norway is concerned. But I don't care about going to my cousin's now that Lady Heriotdale is dead. Heriotdale is almost as great a bore as Curraghmore; besides he is one of those tiresome formalists who think married people ought always to appear as a pair. If I were to go there without Honor, or she without me, he would think we were unhappy. There are people like that, you know; who think a man and woman can scarce breathe happily apart.'

" ' O Lord ! '

" ' Exactly. But instead of some indifferent shooting at Heriotdale's, what do you say to taking a yacht on the Clyde and having a good cruise around the Highland sea-lochs.'

" ' Splendid; and by Jove we might —'

" I would have given a good deal, my dear Jocelyn, to hear what Richard said;

but he spoke in a stage-whisper. Wilfrid laughed lightly, and answered to the effect that man might subdue a continent but could n't repress the old Adam who sat on the box-seat over humanity and held the reins.

"'What do you say to going off this week-end?' Richard resumed. 'We could fix in a few days in London. There 's more than enough to see there in the way of friends, theatres, and all the rest of it.'

"'I 'm ready, my boy. Honor 's a good sort and won't mind. She 's pledged to stay here, or else I would ' —

"'No, no, Wilfrid Adair. When you want whiskey, have whiskey, and when you want whiskey and water have whiskey and water, but for Heaven's sake don't get into the habit of mixing the two merely for the sake of mixing.'

"The wretches seemed to find something amusing in this. My amusement was of a grimmer kind. I know Richard's weak places, and there was a long evening before me.

"Unfortunately I heard no more after this, for they rose and strolled away.

"Well, a certain idea came into my mind straightway. But of this later. I got out of the hammock, and as soon as I reached the house I went to Honor's room. She was writing something, for though she says nothing about it, and is given to an absurd disparagement of herself, she can and does 'write.' But she would not put aside fiction for actuality! In a short time (though the first gong sounded, I admit before I left her) I had told her all, and we had practically resolved on our conspiracy. Also, I may add, I agreed to postpone my revenge on master Dick, — not from mercy, but policy!

"The evening party was dull as usual. Curraghmore discussed John Stuart Mill, while Wilfrid was admiring Honor's profile and Richard was looking at me with those appreciative glances which in a married man of three years' standing are so apt to signify either a request to be proffered erelong (and granted — O weak woman!), or else preparatory conciliation for something done or projected, but in any case requiring to be condoned.

"But a blight lay upon us later: probably

it was John Stuart Mill's philosophy — or the said philosophy as seen through the Reverend James's pince-nez.

"Before we said good-night, Wilfrid Adair remarked casually that, as he had just been telling Honor, he was going away two days hence to spend a week or two with an old friend.

"I tried to catch Richard's eye. He was looking at a copy of one of Guido's inane Madonnas, with an expression of such bland innocence on his face that I doubt if the like of it has been there since he knelt in a little white nightgown at the feet of Mrs. Wester, senior.

"Next morning I was in the breakfast, room before the others. There were newspapers and a circular for Richard, but no letters.

"After the usual chit-chat over the first coffee, Richard suddenly lifted a letter from the table, and with an art that has made me feel more secure for the future (in case he should lose his fortune in Wall Street) announced that he had just heard he would have to go to London for a few days.

"With a ridiculous affectation of surprise, Wilfrid Adair remarked that this would fit in with his own departure on the morrow, and that they could go together.

"Wretches, did they but know that their souls were as strayed camels in the Sahara, and *our* souls as unseen vultures flying high above their foregone prey!

"Honor cracked an egg with an inscrutable smile in her eyes. For myself, I said sweetly: 'I shall go with you as far as Dublin, my dear Richard, as I want some new things, — that is, if you don't invite me to go with you to London. *There's more than enough of friends, theatres, and all the rest of it to see there.*'

"I enjoyed the sudden start that both gave. Fortunately, perhaps, it was due more to the instinctive apprehension of a guilty conscience than to recognition of the fact that their confidences were no longer their own.

"Well, to be brief, the four of us started on the morrow. That day, however, I wrote a long letter to Harry Adair, my younger cousin, and Honor's brother-in-law, — a charming fellow, settled in some shipping agency at Queenstown.

"When we reached Dublin, what do you think my first purchase was? A dress — a hat — gloves — or the like?

"*It was a copy of Montaigne.*

"I gave this to Richard as we said good-by on the Holyhead packet.

"'You will find some pleasant and useful reading there, my dear Dick,' I said, ' Montaigne is a shrewd as well as a charming writer. As you might say, *he lives on the top branch.*'

"Perhaps he thought *that* was my Parthian arrow.

"He would probably change his opinion when he looked into the book, and saw, underlined in the violet ink I often use, two passages : *not* the two he had selected, but these ; the first significant, though not perhaps at first sight so obvious, the second unmistakable : —

"'*Love has compensations that friendship has not.*'

"'*Surely man is a being wonderfully vain, changeable, and vacillating.*'

39

"On the fly-leaf I wrote, —

' *To my dear Richard, on his starting on a tiresome business journey* [with, underneath, the following charming aphorism]:

' *The moral amelioration of man constitutes the chief mission of woman.*'

    (Signed)   ' A FAITHFUL FAILURE.'

"And now about our plan.

"It came to me like a flash of genius. We, also, — that is, Honor and I — are tired of Mountmichael and the Reverend James; we, too, would each enjoy the pleasure of a friendly trip with a dear friend; we, likewise, are fond of the sea, and would dearly love a yachting trip.

"*And a cruise in a yacht on our own account we resolved to have.*

"But the really original suggestion came from Honor.

"'It may or may not be the case, Leonora,' she said to me, 'that we are the first wives who have gone off on a yachting trip without male companionship; but let us be consistent throughout.'

"'How?'

"'Why, by not having a man aboard at all.'

40

"'Not a man at all, Honor Adair!' I exclaimed in amazement. 'But don't you know I mean a *yacht*, not a sailing boat, and *cruise*, not a trip across Dublin Lough!'

"'I do know that. But can't you see that our triumph will be two-fold —not only over our husbands but over men in general —if we can charter a yacht, form a sailing crew of women, and act as our skippers?'

"'You forget, Honor, that I am a mother,' I interrupted severely, 'and that my little Reginald is too young to be left an orphan, well-looked after as he is by Mrs. Wester, senior.'

"'Nonsense, my dear Nora. You and I both know something about yachting; quite as much as Wilfrid does, very likely, and certainly much more than Richard can have had time to pick up. As for the crew, we can commission Harry Adair at Queenstown to select some suitable women, — women who have served on board the Atlantic liners, women who have manned (can we say womaned?) fishing smacks, — women, in a word, who have been brought up by the sea, who are as familiar with the technicalities of sailing as though each was a Will Willyard instead of a bide-i'-th'-house. With a little explanation, good pay, and the fun of the thing, our demand would soon allure a surplus of supply.'

" The idea staggered me, my dear Jocelyn. It was daring; it was delightfully original. It breathed, in a word, of a sweet revenge as well as of a novel joy. But it was — what shall I say? It was revolutionary. That is mild. It was as though the steam should say to the kettle, 'I am tired of this; I want more freedom, — in a word, *you* must now get inside, and be boiled instead of me !'

" But the more I thought of it the more convinced I became that Honor was right. It *would* be so original, — so delightful. In fact her plan added to my idea that touch of irresistible *chic* that the latest fashion gives to a costume.

" ' I yield — I yield,' I cried ; ' I collaborate — I agree — I coincide — I do anything that means you 're a splendid fellow and I 'm another !'

" ' And now, Leonora,' she went on, with

calm triumph, ' we must make up our minds on several matters before we write to Harry Adair to enlist his services. First and fore-most, can we afford this little experience? At the outside I can't put more than £50 or £60 to it.'

" I assured her that the money-part of the business need cause no second thought. I have enough of my own to indulge in a yacht for a whole year if I wish, as *you* know.

" 'Then,' she resumed, ' there is the ques-tion of tonnage, — I mean as to what size of yacht we should have, what crew, what equipment.'

"The tonnage staggered me. I have often been on a yacht, and more than once a long cruise, but I have a poor head for tons. I invariably mix up tonnage and the avoirdupois scale of weight, or else confuse that of ocean steamers and small craft. Remembering that the *Teutonic* is ten thou-sand tons, I thought I would be on the safe side, and so named a twentieth of her tonnage.

" *Five hundred tons!* "

43

"'You should have seen Honor's face. Consternation and pity strove for mastery.

"'My dear Leonora,' she said at last, 'what a glorious imagination you have!'

"I was nettled.

"'Well, Honor, if you think that rather too large let us say half that tonnage.'

"She smiled in that Sphinxian way of hers, and then suggested that we left the matter to Harry Adair with the request that he should find us something over twenty and under five and thirty tons.

"'Now as to the crew.'

"'Let Harry also manage that. You or I can write him in full detail.'

"Well, my dear Jocelyn, to cut short (at this late date) a long story, Harry Adair was written to, acted promptly like the good fellow he is, and informed us in Dublin that he had chartered the yacht *La Belle Aurore*, the property of a gentleman who was anxious to sell her as she lay, "'all found.' We could'nt buy her, but at H's advice we have insured her heavily. Insurance is as serious a matter as making one's will. It depressed me very much at first, but when I realized at last that I could trust in the Insurance Company and not depend solely upon Providence, I felt better.

"While he has been searching for a crew for us we have been busy having yachting costumes, &c., made for us, as well as 'duds' (that is what Harry calls them) for the crew.

"We had endless arguments about the name till we were told by H. A. that *Belle Aurore* must be adhered to meanwhile.

"You should see the caps. They are dears. The *Belle Aurore* on each has every time a new suggestiveness.

"To-morrow the yacht is to arrive in Dublin Lough, and to lie off Bray. There we shall join it. Then —! ! ! ! !

"How you will yearn to hear from me again! Unfortunately, my dear Jocelyn, you will have to practise the virtue of patience!

"Oh, I do hope to-morrow will be fine. It has been wet and dismal enough weather to-day. All evening the wind has moaned like a banshee, and the rain has simply lashed against the windows. Our crew will muster

45

to-morrow. *Of course* they could not accompany the yacht from Queenstown ; yesterday —no, to-day is Friday. Seafaring people are so superstitious. But I do hope they are good sailors. Good-night, dear Jocelyn,

"Your wearied but happy

"LEONORA."

CHAPTER III

SATURDAY, the 21st of July, invaded Dublin with the beauty of unclouded sunshine, borne in upon the wave of a windless calm.

Brown bees hummed about the windows of the Royal Erin Hotel, where the sill-boxes emitted puffs and little clouds of fragrance from clustered mignonette, pansies, and geraniums touched to a vivid and more transparent flame. In circling eddies through the house, and in at the open windows of the lower floors, titillated the exuberant song of the canary in the hall-office of the manageress.

The house-martins that wheeled past gleamed as though they had dyed their wings in the living dawn. The innumerable sparrows were as russet apples turned to the afternoon sun. The flies, those tameless wild dogs of the summer air, shot hither and

47

thither like burnished pellets hurled by the roof-elves and the garden-sprites.

From the street rose a pleasant sound of business. The milkman's cry had a suggestion of sweet-breath'd cows trampling the dewy clover. An Italian who hawked melon-slices and bruised pineapples called his summons with the seductive lure of an evil spirit waylaying the Peri on her way to Heaven's gate. The burly ruffian who shouted, "*Flowers all a-blowin' an' a-growin' !*" had kinship with Ariel, so blithe was his carol, so lifted into sweetness was it by the moving airs of this golden morning.

Fair as was the general seeming, there was (for intending voyagers) a fairer sight within : —

A part-printed, part-written document, in a small oblong frame of black beading, hung upon the wall immediately to the right of the door giving entrance to the breakfast-room.

Hereon was set forth : —

Irish Channel calm. Wind southerly, slight. The day will probably remain fine and warm throughout; hazy towards evening; perhaps thunder, locally along S. and S. E. coasts.

Honor and Leonora were fixt before this announcement, with eyes filled with a happy light.

There could be no question that Providence smiled on them, on their venture. As little question as that the face of man, exemplified in the face of a young commercial traveller, — sole male-guest in the breakfast-room, — beamed upon these two fair ladies, who seemed to him as the very incarnation of the joy and beauty of life.

They were so hopelessly removed from him. Everything betrayed this : perhaps more than anything else, their clear-eyed joy, the unconscious arrogance of happiness.

To the innocent and the narrow-lived is given to eat of the pottage of the bitterness of the things that are.

The young bagman made a poor breakfast. All the hunger seemed to have gone to his eyes.

When the elderly waiter entered with the hot dishes, he looked with not less appreciation, if without a tremor or a quivering under-thought at, No. 33 and 35 First Floor. He was a married man himself, with grown-up daughters, one of them wife to a steward on the Holywell line, the other wed to a tailor and a haberdasher in Dublin. He was therefore in a position to doubly appreciate these nautically clad young women whom "the travelling gent" would as soon have thought of thus prosaically designating as to William it would have occurred to describe them as sea-goddesses.

Each was clad in a tailor-made suit of blue serge, with a white flannel waistcoat, relieved in the instance of Leonora by a blue tie, in that of Honor by one of cardinal red. A sailor's straw hat, with band of blue in the one case, of red in the other, striped with white, gave that crowning touch of sea-smartness which a yachtsman would be the first to appreciate.

As they seated themselves at the little table near the window, they saw two telegrams and a letter awaiting them.

Honor opened the brown envelope addressed to Mrs. Adair.

The missive ran : —

The Norway trip fallen through. Remaining in London week or two, then Scotland. Address, meanwhile, Tamesis Hotel.   WILFRID.

The contents of Mrs. Wester's telegram were the same, with the difference in address :

Detained in London. Can't say how long. Shall write as soon as things are more settled. Address, meanwhile, International Club.

RICHARD.

" Honor," said Leonora, after perusal, " if there's nothing private in it, may I see Wilfrid's telegram ? "

" Certainly. Why ? "

" Men do interest me so much. Richard is as amusing as a pet monkey when it tries to look supernaturally innocent — Ah ! I thought so. *As soon as things are more settled.* My dear Sir, I think my answering telegram will unsettle *you* a little bit more, first."

It took but a minute or so for each to write her reply on the forms submitted by the attentive William. The two telegrams were worded almost identically : —

{ LEONORA
{ HONOR   and I have gone to sea for an indefinite period. Address, meanwhile, " The Yacht *Belle Aurore.*" Ports of call uncertain if any.

{ HONOR
{ LEONORA.

51

With a sigh of relief, Leonora leaned back.

"*Now*, Honor, we can enjoy our breakfast!"

"My dear, you have forgotten the letter from Harry."

"Oh, to be sure I have! how stupid! *There* — what difficult paper to tear! H'm — h'm — *that's* all right — Ah — h! Honor, did you ever hear of a wind *snarling?* That's the expression Harry uses. 'Even now,' he writes, 'when the *Aurore* must be well on her way to you, a nasty sou'wester is snarling round the headlands. The sea is very choppy.'"

"Leonora."

"Yes, dear?"

"I would n't read any more of Harry's reminiscences, if I were you. He means well, no doubt, but when one is about to visit the dentist one does n't rake up one's recollections of every possible unpleasant experience connected with such visits."

"Yes; but — but — *snarling!* I do hope the wind won't *snarl* to-day. Somehow or other it 's much worse than *blowing hard*, or anything of that kind."

" Well, it's not snarling here, that's the main thing. Does Harry make all the rest clear? "

" Absolutely; he has fixt everything, including pay, the signing of the papers, provisioning, and all the rest of it. The particulars about the crew, and various papers, he is sending with Jacob MacMasters, who with two men is bringing the *Aurore* to Bray. I do wish *our* crew had not been so foolish, or — or — pigheaded; after all, the weather has become beautiful, and they might have had a delightful passage."

" What about the snarling, Nora ? "

" Oh, it would have stayed about the headlands, no doubt. But, see, I wonder what Harry means by this: ' I must leave you,' he writes, ' to settle for yourselves the moot point of skippership.' "

" What is the moot point? "

" That's just it. I am glad you are in it also, Honor. I was ashamed to admit that I don't quite know what ' moot ' is. Of course I've often heard of ' moot points.' But I didn't know it was a nautical term."

" But is it, Nora ? "

"Evidently. I—"

Leonora's unfinished sentence was due to the sudden appearance of the elderly William by her side. The waiter had an embarrassed expression, rare to that smug physiognomy which had deferentially or contemptuously fronted so much hotel-visiting humanity.

"What is it, William?"

"If ye please, Mrs. Wester, ma'am, there's a — a — lady, a — a —*pusson*, I should say, who wants to see you immediately. She gives the name of Moriarty. I'm bound to say, ma'am, though she does n't look wiolent, that she calls herself *Capting*, — Capting Moriarty of the *Horoar*, she says, bein' a seafaring man's wife, I suppose."

"Send her up at once, William. We are expecting her. But, William — William — come back a moment! When you announce her, remember to do so simply as *Mrs. Moriarty.*"

"Werry good, ma'am, I quite suspects the situation."

As soon as he had gone, Leonora looked at Honor with a whimsical expression.

"The tragi-comedy begins, my dear!"

"'Come one, come all!' We must now take the bull by the horns, — or, as it would be more apt in the present circumstances to say, take the crew by the curls!"

But here the door opened, and with a loud, nasal, drawling voice the wontedly alert William announced —

"Mrs. Moriarty!"

"*Capting* Moriarty, I tell ye, ye ould astonishment," resounded a hoarse whisper.

"Mrs. Captain Moriarty, late o' the *Hooroar!*" cried William in the high pitched tone of a precentor giving forth "Hark, the herald angels sing!"

"Drop that, ye ondecent absurdity of a man. I'm not a 'late,' not bein' berried yit, praise be to God; an' as for the *Ohrore* I'm first an' earliest an' number wan, an' divil take me if I'll stand quiet when a bald old spalpeen like you, rigmyriggin as a kind o' priest w' your white necktie o' a morning, houlds off, grinnin' like an ape!"

"Oh, what a treasure!" muttered Mrs. Wester below her breath, as she looked with wondering eyes at the stout-figured, ruddy-

faced woman of five and forty or so, clad in
staring blue, with yellow and green bunches
of ribbon slid indiscriminately through the
waist, and with a forlorn stork's nest of a
bonnet of green and blue surmounted by a
flamboyant plume of a color known not of
man nor in Nature. Just then Mrs. Moriarty caught sight of the two ladies, and
advanced to their table clumpily and heavily,
like a bumboat sheering up to a big vessel in
a jumping sea.

"Now, Mrs. Wester, ma'am ! Mrs. Adair,
ma'am ! My respecks to ye both, and I 'm
Nancibel Moriarty, — of which you 'll have
heard afore this from Mr. Adair, o' Queenstown."

"Take a chair, Mrs. Moriarty," said
Honor kindly, seeing that the flustered
woman was distressed by heat and perilously
enclamped stoutness.

"Thank ye, ma'am, an' I will. But I
suppose I 'm capting now, and if it 's all the
same to you, Mrs. Adair, ma'am, and to you
Mrs. Wester, ma'am, I 'd like to have my
rights. There 's them as would like to say
me nay, an' that 's what I 'll stand from no

woman, let alone a Scotch crayture from Greenock, who thinks — ''

'' Now, Mrs. Moriarty, if you 're to sail in the *Belle Aurore*, you must set an example of discipline.''

'' Indade so, Mrs. Adair, if so be as I am right in not misbenaming ye ; an' of that I 'm well aware. O' coorse I know as how you an' Mrs. Wester are over an' above me, captings both, but you must have a capting under ye, or leastwise a chafe officer, an' I wish to clarely understand, wonst an' for all, if I 'm to be capting, or lootennint if ye prefer, an' not that onbendin' arrygint Miss Macfee.''

'' Now, Mrs. Moriarty,'' began Leonora, when she was interrupted by the reappearance of William, —

'' What is it, William ?'' she cried, not having heard what he had just announced.

Clearing his throat, and opening the door so as to make way for a new-comer, he repeated his words, —

'' Another lady to see you and Mrs. Adair, ma'am. Miss Macfee, likewise, o' the *Hooroar !* ''

57

Honor and Leonora looked at each other. An embarrassed smile fled like a spent fugitive across either face.

Mrs. Moriarty turned. If the tall, gaunt, bony-featured, grim-visaged woman who had entered had looked at her irate rival she might well have quailed before the wrath and indignation struggling for mastery on that honest if empurpled face.

"Em I speakin' to the leddies Mrs. Adair and Mrs. Wester?"

The voice was singularly low in pitch and soft in intonation. One would expect, from Miss Macfee's exterior, a rasping or at least a harsh and dissonant utterance. She had a Fifeshire mien, an east-country gauntness and grimness; but when she spoke she betrayed that she was of the West country, and that her breed was Highland.

Leonora leaned across the table. As she did so, she upset an egg-cup.

"Well, Miss Macfee, what do you want?"

"I'se be tellin' ye that in a minnit, mem; but if ye'll allow me I'll just clean up that egg."

With an abrupt gesture, she snatched a

napkin from the hand of William, who had approached, and hovered near, one-part attention, three-parts curiosity.

Miss Macfee was just in time. The egg had broken; in another moment the yolk would have smeared Leonora's cuff and sleeve.

Instinctively, Mrs. Moriarty knew that her rival had gained a point. She herself was nearer Mrs. Wester, nearer the spot of the accident; and had made no sign. Readiness is one of the first qualifications of a skipper.

" Drat that egg," she exclaimed.

" Mrs. Moriarty ! "

The culprit grew more apoplectic. She looked appealingly at the two ladies.

" God knows, ma'am, I meant, no disrespeck to the egg or — or — to you, ma'am — though if you 'll be so swate as to allow me to say so, ma'am, and ladies both, I think as how by the look of it, or what I saw of it before this woman here spiled that nate new napkin with it, it would have been better poached ; but anyways, as I was saying —"

Honor interrupted with a smile and a gesture.

"That will do, Mrs. Moriarty. Now, tell
Mrs. Wester and myself, what you and Miss
Macfee have come here for. Why are you
not at Bray, on board the *Belle Aurore* ?"

"The other ladies — "

"The crew, if you please, Mrs. Moriarty."

"Yes, ma'am, to be sure. As I was
sayin', the crew is now there ; but on the
way up from Cork Miss Macfee here put on
airs as if she were a capting-born, which was
more than I could stand, not from two sich
women as her, let alone my bein' a widder
an' the daughter of a gintleman if ever there
was one, an' as well known in tallow-
chandling as the Quane among thrones and
dominions."

"What were the airs about?"

"About bein' capting of the *Bellowroar*.
Indade, ma'am, I was as put about for your
sakes as for my own. Ridicilus thing, says
I to myself, to be so presooming when I, a
widder, an' — "

"Yes, yes, the daughter of a gintleman, —
we all know that, Mrs. Moriarty. But tell us
who ever gave you to understand that either
you or Miss Macfee was to be captain of

the *Belle Aurore?* I'm sure Mr. Adair never said anything of the kind?"

"It was 'er airs, ma'am; the way she set 'erself. Indade, Mrs. Wester, ma'am, you would need to have seen with your own blessed eyes —"

"One moment, Leonora," whispered Honor, as she turned to Miss Macfee; "Now, you tell us what this is all about."

"Least said soonest mended, mem," said the Scotchwoman dryly; "this woman's a puir dementit fule."

A shout of laughter broke from both Honor and Leonora. There was contagion in that blithe music.

A smile, sad as tribulation, grim as poverty, flickered like a chilly dawn upon the barren landscape of Miss Macfee's face. The purple glow in that of Mrs. Moriarty waned. A quiver went through the unwieldy body; the flaring plume above the green-blue atrocity shook like a reed in the wind. The broad expansive grin that followed was like the rush of the tide across a shallow lagoon.

Suddenly a snigger came from William.

Looking in the narrow wall-mirror to her right, Leonora saw that the young commercial was silently laughing.

There was an indrawn breath as if Glee were choking. At the very moment came from the street the song of the itinerant minstrel, —

    " Oh who would sail the wild, wild sea,
      Brave mariners one and all !
        'ners one — and — aw-w-ll-ll !
      The wild sec-ee-ee,
      The lonely see-ee-ee ! "

Honor sat back in her chair. Tears were in her eyes; suffocation in her throat. She shook, — at the mercy of the wild folly of things in general.

Leonora's case was scarce better. But with an effort she controlled herself.

"Oh, how funny ! But Honor, do be quiet ! And now, Mrs. Moriarty and Miss Macfee, since we 've all forgotten what we were disputing about, don't let us begin again. You two shake hands; yes, yes, I insist upon it !— There now, that 's right, though it 's enough to make an angel weep to see the way you do it ! Now I tell you what you've got to do. You've got to obey orders. That's all. There are no commanding officers on board the *Belle Aurore* except Mrs. Adair and myself. We are the captain. The crew consists of the non-commissioned officers and three seamen —"

"Seawomen," Honor interposed.

"Yes; three seawomen and two non-commissioned officers, respectively the cook and the steward. Mrs. Moriarty, you are non-commissioned officer Cook; Miss Macfee, you are non-commissioned officer Steward."

"Excuse me one moment, Mrs. Wester, ma'am — I mean Capting; but which is First Officer, — me or Miss Macfee?"

Leonora started, perplexed. With nautical alertness Honor came to the rescue.

"Mrs. Wester and I have already settled that point. You are *both* first officer. You, Mrs. Moriarty, in the cuddy and forepart of the yacht; you, Miss Macfee, in the cabin and the afterpart."

"And in the case o' death, mutiny, wounds, starvation, fire, wisittation o' God, an' —"

"In all such instances the joint command

63

will devolve upon Miss Macfee and yourself,
— that is, if the ' visitation of God ' be upon
us and not upon *you*; in which latter case
we undertake to bury you with first-officer
honors."

This concession had a marked effect upon
Mrs. Moriarty. She took on the pleased
mien of a diplomatist who had gained her
point.

" One word more, Captings both, if you
will *he*xcuse me. Supposin', wich the Holy
Virgin forefend, that me an' Miss Macfee has
to take the command, an' if she should be
havin' a fancy to sail to Scotland an' I should
be thinkin' it my dooty to be back at Cork,
how 's the crayture to be driven to market
on *that* day? "

"Odd man out," thus Honor, oracularly.

" *What*, ma'am — Capting, I 'm manin'? "

" I should have said odd woman out," resumed Honor, calmly. " There are five of
you all together. We shall make Bridget
O'Leary second non-commissioned officer.
Whoever one sides with will have an acting
majority. That leaves Jane Lanigan and
Mary Murtagh, besides Polly Jones, the cabin

64

boy — I mean, girl; Polly does n't count.
Lanigan will be the first watch; Murtagh
the second. Polly will see to the striking
of the bells; also to varnishing our shoes.
And now, Mrs. Moriarty and Miss Macfee,
be so good as to go on board as soon
as you can. We shall follow in an hour or
so. Ah, by the way, of course you understand that there is to be no 'mistressing' and
'missing' on board the *Belle Aurore*. Mrs.
Wester and I will be Captain Wester and
Captain Adair. You will be Moriarty and
Macfee."

The two women moved slowly away; the
Scot like a shifted tide-pole, the lady from
Cork in the manner of a Dutch sloop in a
heavy sea. William piloted them.

At the door Mrs. Moriarty turned.

"Captings dear," she cried, insinuatingly,
"could n't you make it *Mrs*. Moriarty and
Miss Macfee, seein' as how your honors have
just agreed to us as bein' first orficers?"

"You have let yourself in for it, Honor!"
Leonora whispered, as she raised her napkin to hide the irrepressible laughter to which
she had begun to give way as soon as the

visitors' backs were turned. "You *must* concede something!"

"Halt!" exclaimed Honor, in the tone of a martinet. Simultaneously she was conscious that she had used the wrong word. She would have died rather than admit her mistake.

"Halt!" she repeated. "Mrs. Moriarty, your name in full, your Christian name?"

"Florence. That's my Christian name, Capting. Me ould nonsensicle fhather baptized me Dan'l O'Connell as well; but barrin' it's not bein' a woman's name at all at all, I don't call it a Christian name, an' so I'm always called Florence by them as has the right, an' Florrie by——"

"That will do, please. And your name, Miss Macfee?"

"Janet."

"Very good. If you do not like 'Moriarty' and 'Macfee' we can call you Florence and Janet. Think it over and let us know when we come aboard. Good evening! William, shut the door; there is a draught."

When the door was closed, Honor and

Leonora sat back and gave way for a few moments to a burst of joyous laughter.

" Honor, me darlint, as First Officer Moriarty might say, if we never got beyond Dublin Lough, this experience is worth all the thought and trouble we have had ! *What* a couple of women ! The fair and corpulent Florrie, the thin and grim Janet ! And oh, that excruciating dress in the latest Cork wharfside fashion, that awful, awful bonnet ! "

" Was n't it fascinating, Nora ? — horribly, wildly fascinating ? Never have I seen such an atrocity before, never can I hope (and indeed I don't !) to see its like again ! "

Something in Honor's manner attracted her companion's closer attention. She was less reserved than the occasion warranted. There was in her mien the look of a beautiful mare when she knows she is admired and is about to be caressed. A glance at the mirror at her side explained all. Therein she caught a glimpse of the young commercial traveller, eating with his knife, it is true, but with his eyes fixed in a hungry wistful stare upon the beauty of Honor. A living admiration filled his eyes, the unmistakable reflection of his thoughts.

In the same glass Honor had made the like discovery. Leonora looked mischievously at her friend. Then, leaning forward, she recited in a low voice.

> " Kinds hearts are more than coronets,
> And simple faith than Norman blood ! "

Honor looked at her. Amazement was in her gaze. Then, as she divined Leonora's malicious smile, and caught the rapid flirt of her glance towards the admiring phantom-youth in the mirror, the lovely dark eyes took on a violet dusk. Her faint wild-rose bloom deepened into a fugitive flush.

With an abrupt gesture she rose, and dropped her napkin on her plate. Mrs. Wester rose also ; calmly folded and ringed her napkin ; glanced amusedly at her friend ; and, with a slight inclination as she passed the suffering male, went towards the door, opened it, and disappeared.

Honor moved to the window. The view was enticing, no doubt. The way of the wind was studiously observed by her. She

watched the flirtations of the sparrows. A
brown bee, flying idly by to a window-box
as yet unrifled, sang a woodland song. The
lyric note was abroad.

With a sigh she half-turned, but changed
her mind. The bee had lost itself among
the mignonette on the neighboring sill; the
sparrows had flown high and low, love's
young dream already dissipated. She was
not thinking of either. She was unfastening
the cream-hued tea-rose she wore at her
neck.

What was Leonora doing, she wondered;
a conscious wonderment. Suddenly she
turned. With a well-feigned start of surprise she betrayed her astonishment at the
unexpected absence of her friend. She
walked rapidly past the table, her eyes intent
upon the door, ajar but Williamless. The
young man who had worshipped her across
his ham and eggs, who had for her forgotten
time, commissions, distractions innumerable,
half rose, flushed awkwardly, bowed more
awkwardly still. It was one of the moments
of his life. Honor did not know it, or she
would have vouchsafed him more than the

glance she shot at him for the flying fraction of a second. Still less did he know it. If he had, he would probably have sat still and gasped. Thus jocundly go the high emotions, oftener than not contrary to all novelistic procedure and convention.

In this fashion Mrs. Adair disappeared, from that room for good no doubt, from that gaze forever. She left behind her a deathless memory, and a perishable cream-white tea-rose.

CHAPTER IV

W HEN Mrs. Wester and Mrs. Adair
stepped from the car at Bray, and
found themselves in sight of the sea, they
stared inland.

They had been admired on the tram-car.
Possibly, too, some rumor of their novel
adventure had got abroad. The conductor
had whispered to the middle-aged marine
gentleman with a straw hat, a white waistcoat, tan shoes, beady eyes, and a fleshy
nose. He had smirked. If the information
had been a word of admiration only for
those two spruce and most winsomely nautical young women, he would, as both ladies
instinctively and indignantly divined, have
ogled. His smirk meant amusement. What
could this summer-resort limpet be amused
at were it not by the idea of a cruise of fair
women, conducted on the lines of the most
pronounced sexual independence?

He, in his turn, had winked to a pale youth sitting opposite to him. Thenceforth two gooseberry-eyes had dwelt waterily now upon Mrs. Adair now upon Mrs. Wester.

Further, he of the beady eyes and oiled locks had audibly confided somewhat to his neighbor, a horsey man with an enormous skull scarf-pin, a checkered blue and buff waistcoat, pelican legs, a small round billy-cock tipped sideways, a face mottled like a boiling lobster and veined protuberantly, and with shifty eyes that rarely surmounted the bridge of his nose. Leonora had overheard certain words: "that yacht," "girls," "rum uns," and "devilish queer lot."

A hint to Honor, half glance half oral, had been enough, as the car reached its terminus.

Thus it was that the two ladies had turned their eyes away from the sea. Thirty yards beyond them, on an islet between the straits of West Road and Little West Road, stood the aristocratic, exclusive, expensive, and generally delectable private hotel known as Londonderry Mansion.

An idea flashed across Leonora's mind.

"Come, Honor," she said, in the distinct

tone she generally reserved for the close of arguments with Mr. Wester; "we'll have early luncheon at the Londonderry, and then go for our walk afterwards."

The ruse was successful. The loafers who had strolled up, the marine-limpet, the watery-eyed youth, the shifty bookmaker, one and all dispersed. No, said the manageress of the Londonderry, a few minutes later, she had received no word from either a Mrs. Adair or a Mrs. Wester. "Very likely," she added, "they will be here this evening."

"Possibly," Leonora remarked; "if so, we'll be sure to call again. Good morning."

The way was clear. A couple of hundred yards distant a small boat glided upon the beach. A dozen interested spectators clustered about its bows. As Honor and Leonora drew near they noted that this unnecessary gathering was augmented by a thirteenth individual. The limpet was true to his instinct.

Both adventurers caught their breath. Moral courage, or the lack of it, causes more perturbation to some people than the advent of a bull on a lonely road does to others. Those, however, who suffer from moral courage generally disguise it; often so effectively that it is never made evident.

The two ladies became absorbed in the beauty of the sea. Each stopped, entranced. Honor raised an arm, and pointed vaguely ocean-ward. " Yes," said Leonora nervously, looking in the opposite direction; " it is beautiful, beautiful."

There was a slight commotion in the group about the small boat. Honor saw this out of the corner of an eye.

" Nora, what shall we do? We can't stand here in this ridiculous fashion looking at nothing as though we had never seen it before! Besides, there are at least half a dozen boatmen who have espied us, and are bearing down upon us like crabs."

Mrs. Wester hesitated; but at that moment a laugh decided them. It stung them into quiet self-possession.

The spilt noise — for to speak of so coarse and raucous an outbreak as laughter would be to flatter — came from the human limpet. Strange that so alien a sound should cause a light as of blue steel in the eyes of two blithe young women.

As they turned and walked towards the boat, the man advanced. He raised his hat with a jerk. Leonora noticed that he gripped the brim so tightly that the straw bent. For all his audacity, then, he was nervous.

"Ladies," began this male, smirking —

"Thank you," Honor interrupted, in a voice which fell as against a frosty air, so chill was it; "we have no need of your services."

"Services, Miss? Ma'am, I should say, perhaps? I am a gentleman, and don't want to serve you or any one, — that is, you know, in the way you mean. Or perhaps you don't mean that, but — oh, I see! Forgive me, Miss — Ma'am — But please allow me to give you a few tips. Live down here. Well known. Great boating man. Doubt if that yawl out there is in proper trim. Go over there with you if you like. No intrusion, ladies. Glad to do anything for a glance from lovely eyes — eh? ah?"

"Will you be good enough, sir, to mind your own business?"

"Ah, married; I thought so. I know the tone of voice. But see here —" The man had not much experience of women, or rather he judged all women by the females of his species.

The quiet look in the eyes, the slight curl of contempt in the lips, of Mrs. Adair and her companion, actually impressed him. He stood back, momentarily shamefaced. When he saw the grin on the face of the idlers by the boat, he scowled.

Virtuous indignation is often lit by the match of another's discomfiture. When the gaily-bedaubed offence began with, " Well, you need not be so 'aughty; I know girls as good as you who—" an elderly mariner stepped forward, and in a voice husky with emotion and gin told him not to annoy the purty young ladies who might surely go out for a sail without bein' badgered by the likes o' him.

The mariner was tall and wiry, but the interloper saw his opportunity in the obfuscation of gin. A duel of words of the mud and debris of language, if not actually a conflict of blows, seemed imminent.

The creature took a step back, the better to spit its venom. Alas, one of those jaunty spat-bedecked feet caught in a slit in a rock. There was a stagger upon the slimy sea-moss; a cry; a coarse oath; a fallen straw-hat in a pool of anemones which hailed a mighty brother: and then a heavy recumbent figure that slid, that wriggled, that half rose and fell prostrate again, till it found itself in that tepid shallow bath wherein the straw-hat already lay submerged, bappy with the ooze.

Long before the sputterings on the one hand and the loud and unrestrained jubilation on the other were over, Honor and Leonora were by the dingey, almost unnoticed.

In the small boat they descried two jaunty figures: females both, and stout; but glorious as the Stars and Stripes on Independence Day, for each was raimented in an immense jersey of red, striped with white, while on each ample bosom suspended an azure star. A white straw hat with scarlet band, and with blue star in the forefront, completed the marine nattiness of each nereid.

"Harry Adair has let his imagination run riot," Mrs. Wester murmured as she moved steadily forward, nodded with the ease of one accustomed to the high seas and piratical costumes, and laid hand upon the bows of the boat. The tide was full and the dingey was off keel. The punt nosed the pebbly slope like a terrier, but her stern swung clear.

The two seawomen saluted. The ceremony was less impressive than it was meant to be, for the upswung oars met midway with a clash. They came down waveringly, amidst muttered objurgations. Fortunately, further reprisals were postponed.

Leonora's presence of mind did not desert her. With a glance at Honor she remarked, loudly enough to be overheard : —

"That is our American fashion. It is different from yours, I think?"

"Yes," replied Honor, with smiling malice, "oars are expensive with us."

Mrs. Wester's point was not lost upon the two members of the *Belle Aurore's* crew. They smiled sympathetically. The *rapport* was established : each felt to the other as a woman and a sister.

The two ladies stepped lightly into the dingey. When they had seated themselves, the boat now, like a typical Hibernian beauty, with a *nez retroussé*, bobbed blithely from the shore. A scattered cheer came from the onlookers. A tiny girlet, wading naked to where her white dress was humped above her sun-browned little stomach, making her seem like a froth-crowned pot of ale, shrieked excitedly.

"What on earth is that child yelling about?" Mrs. Wester asked anxiously, fears of ferocious lobsters and imprisoned infantile toes perturbing her mind.

"Och, 't is only bekas' your sleeve 's thrailin' in the wather, Mr. Capting, mum!"

The explanation came from "stroke."

Leonora rescued the extreme of her sleeve; then, looking at the late speaker, asked her her name.

"Bridget O'Leary, if ye plase, mum — Capting, I mane."

"And you?"

This to the other, who in her mingled excitement and interest had forgotten to keep time with "Stroke."

"Mary Murtagh!"

79

The words were propelled as by blasting powder. Heat and exertion already threatened the fair, blue-eyed, moon-faced Mary. Bridget was small and dark, but rotund also, and as she moved to and fro with her oar, her beady black eyes fixed upon her "capting's," her bosom swoln with pride and tight-lacing so that the ruddy jersey was drawn to its extreme of tautness, she seemed like a gigantic robin-redbreast.

"Well, Bridget, and you, Mary, this is Mrs. Adair, and I am Mrs. Wester. Captain Adair and Captain Wester, you know. I hope we'll all get on well together."

"May I be so bold as to ask a question, Capting?"

"Yes."

"Is Mr. Macmasters comin' wid us?"

"Mr. Macmasters? Ah, to be sure, Jacob Macmasters. No, Bridget, certainly not."

Robin-Redbreast sighed.

Honor saw disappointment. She reminded Miss O'Leary of the Female Constitution which they were there to uphold.

"And why are you disappointed?" she added.

"I ask your parding, Captings both. I was thinkin' o' the childher, little Pathrick an' little Phelim. Pore things, if they sud be left ahlone in the world an' them twins too, worse luck, though by the grace o' God!"

"Patrick and Phelim? Who are Patrick and Phelim?"

"They 're the twins, Capting Adair."

"Whose twins?"

"Faith, an' they 're mine: and both as purty an' —"

"Yours?"

"Shure. I —"

"Bridget O'Leary, you are entered on the — on the — in the *Belle Aurore's* books as Miss O'Leary?"

"Well, Capting, it 's thrue an' it 's not thrue."

In her eagerness to explain, Miss O'Leary ceased rowing, and leaned forward. Miss Murtagh, embarrassed under Leonora's eye and a consciousness of impending doom, made up for the lapse by a feverish energy. The dingey lurched and swung round.

Mrs. Wester and Mrs. Adair faced the shore

again. Neither had time to exclaim before the bows surged towards England. A swirl, and the *Belle Aurore* again confronted them.

"Stop, woman! Stop, Mary Murtagh," cried the two skippers simultaneously; Mrs. Wester adding severely, "Do you think we want to be drowned in a spinning-top?"

"And now, Bridget O'Leary, explain," resumed Honor.

"Well, ma 'am,—Captings, I mane,—I 'm not exactly a miss, Pathrick an' Phelim bein' my twin bhoys, an' the handsomest pair your honours ever saw though it's I as says it. An' as to my not bein' Mrs. instead of Miss, well Capting Adair, mum, an' Capting Wester, I 've 'ad my misfhortin' like manny another pore woman."

"You are not married, and yet you have twins, O'Leary?"

"'T is thrue. I 'm not denyin' it. Cork 's a bad place, though it 's I as says it, an' Cork-born an' Cork-bred at that."

Honor looked at Leonora, who looked at Mary Murtagh, who looked in settled dismay at the nearest thole-pin.

Mrs. Wester saw the need of balm.

"Well, Bridget, we are very sorry to hear this. Is — eh — is Mr. O'Leary —"

"His name 's Denis O'Flaherty, an' he 's in Chiney now, worse luck."

"Is he likely to marry you when he comes back?"

"He 's sworn it by all the saints. Bless the bhoy, — an' a third steward he is aboard the *Cawnpore* — he wrote me from some haythen port to say that if it was a bhoy, an' I christened it Denis, he 'd not be mane enough to hould back the Flaherty from the spalpeen's name."

"But — but —"

"To be shure, Capting. I know what your honour 's after sayin'. But you see I wasn't to know there wud be *two* on them. An' when I saw them both I cud a' cried my eyes out for bein' so onsartain as to what to do. Bein' twins I cud n't call one o' the childher Denis, for 't would be moighty onfair to the other. Mebbe Mr. O'Flaherty would n't acknowledge him, an' I cud n't bhear to part them. He said 'a bhoy an' to be called Denis;' an' shure I know him

83

well enough to see how he 'd look if I told him there was two in the same poke. ' *One* bhoy, an' Denis at that,' he would say; 'a bargain 's a bargain, an' I 'm off. I 'll take wan, an' you with him, but no Christing man ever 'ad two sons passed on him under wan name.' An' that 's how it is, Captings dear. An' so as Pathrick 's his father's name, an' Phelim that o' the friend that first brought us together (an' a jealous man Denis was till Phelim went as a stoker on the *Buffalo*, in the Phillydelfy line), I thought I 'd hould over the name o' Denis till the next toime, — an' please God may it be a bhoy, for gurls — "

"That will do, Bridget."

A sob came from the oarswoman. The brine in the sea was increased by a few drops that rolled from rubicund cheeks.

Silence prevailed in the stern sheets.

" 'Tis a misfhortin, Capting Wester an' Capting Adair; 't is a misfhortin, an' I 'm not denying of it. It comes when least expected an' least wanted, like measles or croup wi' childher. We pore women has a lot to bear. Mary Murtagh herself 'll be tellin' as you — "

"What! not you too, Mary?" Leonora cried in alarm.

"No — no — ma'am — Captings!" Miss O'Leary interjected, "I'm not manin' that Mary has twins, nor even the half o' that number; though for shure atween her an' me an' the north wind, to say nothing at all o' Mr. Ned Sullivan o' the Customs, I —"

An abrupt thrust in the back deprived O'Leary of the wind that upbore her eloquence. An altercation loomed. Mrs. Adair took prompt action, and the situation was saved.

"Row on!" she exclaimed. "Murtagh, you row the harder, the tide is against you. Now then, time, keep time."

Once more the dingey sped on its bobbing way. In a few minutes it was alongside the trim, cleanly-built, swan-buoyant yacht, whose shape and air of rakish distinction had delighted the eyes of the two friends who had chartered her for their cruise.

The *Aurore* lay upon the water with that air of delicate pleasure which all well-built and well-kept yachts have. She was a yawl of about thirty tons. Her lines had a long, unbroken sweep, which made her seem lower in the water than she was. Black, but for a rim of gold, she was like a huge bird winged for flight, but still afloat.

Both Honor and Leonora knew enough of yachts and yachting to appreciate not only the beauty but the admirable trim of the vessel, which they scrutinized with growing gratification and pleasure as they drew near. The half-furled mainsail was white, but with the true whiteness of foam, and not of mill-dust. The yards and spars were clean. With nothing, from anchor-tip to helm, could fault have been found.

They swung up to the port side, where the gangway was suspended. There, Jacob Macmasters, a short, elderly man, with an Ibsenitish volume of outbrushed hair, wherein beard and whisker and the upper jungle combined in one tangled ash-gray wilderness, awaited them, hat in hand. Mrs. Wester was the first to rise. Mary and Bridget were not adepts with the oars, and they forgot to allow for the wash between the dingey and the yacht. The result was that Leonora was put to the rack. She had grasped the rope-gangway, and had clung desperately to it as the boat drifted back. In a second or two she knew that either she would have to let go, and fall head-foremost into the sea, or cling on and find herself to her waist atrail in the water.

The elderly Jacob came to the rescue. Even in that crucial moment she noticed that he did not smile. She was grateful. It flashed across her mind that a noble gravity differentiates man from woman.

He grasped her by the wrists. Half lifting, half pulling, he served two ends; for her feet had caught in the gunwale, and as Jacob Macmasters drew her backward the dingey followed till it bobbed against the side once more.

A minute later Leonora was on deck, gasping, racked, indignant, confused, stricken with unlaughed laughter, and, above all, conscious of garments twisted, necktie awry, the dainty straw-hat rakishly lop-sided.

CHAPTER V

" MORNIN', mum."
" Good morning, Mr. Macmasters."
Already the ordeal was over. Discipline
had triumphed. Jacob Macmasters, still hat
in hand, stood smileless; smileless, a yard
or so away, First-Officer Moriarty and First-
Officer Macfee; smileless, the third A. B.
in the crew, Jane Lanigan, a strapping lass
of twenty, with red hair, a starry profusion
of freckles, and a cast in the eyes that made
each optic seem wildly ogling the other.
Only a very small and young smile hovered
about the round face of Polly Jones, the
cabin-girl. The child had something of the
appearance and much of the stolidity of
the average suet-dumpling. Small and frail
as this sole smile was, it flattened gradually
into the inane whence it came.

As soon as Honor had joined Leonora,
Murtagh and O'Leary were about to follow.
Macmasters, however, bade them wait.

"A happy voyage to you, mum; and to you, mum, likewise."

"Thank you, Mr. Macmasters. This lady is Mrs. Adair. I am Mrs. Wester. We are sorry you are not to accompany us, but Mr. Harry Adair will already have told you about our plan."

"Yes, mum."

"Perhaps you could stay for an hour and give us some hints?"

"Sorry, mum, but I've got to be in Dublin before two o'clock. Goin' back to Cork in the 'Arp o' Hearin',"

"In the — ah, yes, to be sure. Well, we thank you for bringing the *Belle Aurore* round so promptly."

"Bless your 'art, mum, she comed herself; she's the devil to go. She up skirts, dangles her ankles, and afore you knows were she is she's dancing a jig a mile away."

"Re-a-ally," remarked Leonora, vaguely, to whom the answer had been directed. "How interesting! But I hope she's — eh — ah —easy to manage?"

"Ay, ay, mum, easy enough in fair weather."

" But in bad weather ? "

An ominous silence followed. Jacob Macmasters wiped his mouth with his sleeve, as though removing the invisible froth of imaginary beer. Honor thought Leonora a poor tactician. With a smile she said that they were both too good sailors and too much accustomed to yachting to mind bad weather : in fact they rather liked it. Only, if Mr. Macmasters thought the *Belle Aurore* was not easily manageable with a high sea running, it would be as well if he were to specify her several virtues and vices.

" Keep your heye on her, mum. When the sea jumps *she* jumps. She 's a one-er to jump."

" Does she roll ? "

" Well, she *can* roll. I don't know as I was ever in a wessel that rolled so much, — for her size, I' m meaning. I 've seen her roll so that —." But here Leonora interrupted.

" Mr. Macmasters, you know the signs of the weather. What kind of evening are we going to have ? "

" Baddish, I 'm fearin'. Indeed, I ain't just sure — "

" Ah, quite so. Now you see, Mr. Mac-masters, the glass is good, the sky is clear, the water is just as blue and white as good sea-water should be. Don't you think you are croaking a little ? "

Mr. Macmasters stared meditatively. Then he looked from Leonora to Honor, and from Honor to First-Officers Moriarty and Mac-fee, and from them to Polly Jones. There-after his slow gaze embraced the rigging, drowsed upon the cabin-hatch, slept upon the wheel.

" Well, Mr. Macmasters ? "

The mariner turned. There was that in his eye which hinted explosion. Explosion it was : laughter, — deep, gurgling, asth-matic, rum-hoarsened, genuine laughter.

" Hexcuse me, Mrs. Wester, mum ! Hex-cuse me, Mrs. Adair, mum ! " he stuttered. " I 'm took that way sometimes. It 's the salt o' the sea as does it, — the salt o' the sea by night, when the rheum 's about, an' there ain't no way out of it."

A polar breath was in Honor's voice as she spoke : —

" We shall not detain you longer, Mr.

91

Macmasters. And — ah, Macmasters, I hope the *Harp of Erin* will have a good passage, for I fancy you are rather unaccustomed to rough weather at sea. Good-day!"

The dart pierced a thickish hide. The crew grinned. With difficult dignity the late captain nodded farewell. On the face of First-Officer Macfee there was a frosty smile. It aggravated him. As he disappeared over the side of the yacht, to the alarm of Murtagh and O'Leary, who had been indulging in a lively argument anent the recent revelations as to the twins, he turned.

"Man, Macfee," he said confidentially, "it's no your beauty that you're paid for!"

First-Officer Moriarty, forgetful of discipline, laughed. Seeing the frowning reproof on the face of each of her captains, she repented, and cried imperatively, "Order! Order, there"!

With that Mr. Macmasters was all but gone. Doubtless he thought he had planted his arrow, and could go in peace. But then yachts may have unexpected furniture, and Parthian shafts were here.

Walking to the taffrail, Miss Macfee called

to the seawomen: "Tak tent how you row there! Nae splashin'! Hae a care o' Jacob, puir wee man!"

Harmony was restored on the *Belle Aurore*. Obviously, captains and officers had resource. With resource, — well, the world should note how successfully wives at sea could dispense with their adjuncts!

"And now, Honor, let us go below."

"Yes,' replied Captain Adair, with a precautionary glance, as of one to the manner born, at the masts and furled mainsail; "we may as well take a look round."

The moment they were below, they were in each other's arms. It was delightful to be there, they two, on the *Belle Aurore*, with a calm sea and favoring breeze, and with, for haven, the blue waters of the Port of Adventure.

"Oh, Captain, my Captain," laughed Mrs. Wester, reminiscent of words of Walt Whitman's, "Is not this simply heavenly? And *what* a crew we've got! Oh, it's too delicious! If only they know anything at all, we'll arrive — we'll arrive somewhere! What a jolly little cabin!"

A dainty sea-nest it was, indeed. Dark polished oak-panelling, a narrow table covered with a snow-white cloth, a swing-rack supplied with crystal as clear-shining as hope ; and then, to right and left — " to starboard and larboard, Honor " ! said Mrs. Wester — two of the most charming tiny rooms that were ever afloat, each with a bunk in it that looked like a captured snowdrift. The hangings, the fittings, everything was delightful. Deep sighs of content floated hither and thither wafted onward by little breaths of laughter.

" Honor ! "

" Yes, Leonora ? "

" There are people who say life is n't worth living ! "

" They have never been to sea."

" There are people who say there is nothing worth doing ! "

" They have never seen a *Belle Aurore*."

" There are women who say marriage is a failure ! "

" They have never given their spouses the slip ! "

" Oh, Honor ! "

" Oh, Nora ! "

At that moment Polly Jones entered, coming down the cabin stair as though she were of india-rubber, and had to follow the rule of her kind and bump from side to side.

" Please 'm ! "

" Polly," said Mrs. Wester, severely, " don't stare at nothing. If you say *please 'm* you must mean one *'m* in particular."

" Yes 'm, please 'm ! Miss Macfee,'m, wants to know if you 'd like anything, 'm ? "

" Yes, Polly. Let me see, Honor, do you like your grog neat ? "

" Yes." There was no smile on Mrs. Adair's face. The cabin-girl was impressed. Here were sailors indeed !

" After all " — and with what careless sangfroid was it said — " after all, Honor, we 'd better see if Moriarty knows how to make tea. Polly, tell Miss Macfee we 'll have tea."

"Yes, Capting, 'm."

" Don't say *'m,* Polly."

" No, 'm."

" And look here, Polly, eh — ah — confound your eyes ! " broke in Honor, with her

95

own bright lights a-twinkle like stars, — "tell First-Officer Macfee that immediately after tea we shall have the roll-call."

"Yes, Capting Adair, 'm."

Whereupon the child vanished. The forecastle would soon echo to the rumor of unstinted admiration.

But when she was gone, Mrs. Wester looked reproachfully at her friend. "Honor — you are beautiful, but you 're a — well, a dear sea-donkey!"

"Why, O Wisdom?"

"Heavens, Captain Adair, you don't have a *roll-call* on board a yacht, or at sea. Roll-calls are for — eh, ah, — the land-forces — Lady Butler's paintings — and — and so on."

"Never mind, Nora, we can adopt what we choose. What 's the good of having a yacht to ourselves, and being wives in exile, if we can't have the privilege of doing and saying what our husbands would shiver at?"

"That 's true, dear. Ah, here comes our first officer — our twin-first officer — with the tea. Thank you, Macfee — Miss Macfee — that will do nicely. Let me see, what are these?"

"These are scones, mem. Mrs. Moriarty mebbe doesna ken sae much as she thinks she does, but she can mak buttered scones."

Was there ever so delightful a tea, though taken so early in the afternoon, and only with two wives for company? Was it Honor, or was it Leonora whose rapture first became lyric? An intoxication lay in that brew of Cork-supplied 'blend,' nay lurked in the diluted cream which First-Officer Moriarty had chastened for the good of the captains, for whom too rich a diet could not be good, on the eve of a sea-voyage.

After all, was it the cream, the tea? Or was it the keen breath of ocean, or the laughter of the foam-crested wavelets slapping one against the other in the sunshine?

Or was it the sunshine in the brain, the sunny laughter of life in the hearts of two happy young women? What intoxication is like that, — the sweet delirium of happy life?

It was with a sigh that Honor drank the last mouthful from her cup, — "quaffed the foaming bowl" would be more romantic, of course, but less exact, and if this chronicle has any value, it is that of absolute veracity. So, not the bowl — though, indeed, a compromise might have been effected with the sugar-bowl — but the cabin-cup, that is quite as intoxicating, and is wed to laughing gossip and the rout of the azure imps, — sole vagabonds of the blue-devil cohort that dare stray near youth in its prime.

"Nora," she said, in a voice that would have made the heart of the young commercial in the Dublin hotel palpitate as no unexpected windfall could have done, "Nora asthore, *oh, it is good!*"

"Mrs. Adair, your sentiments do you honor. But now I'm going to unpack. There is no reason why we should not be comfortable in case that 'snarling' comes on, which Harry spoke about."

"Right; but we need n't expect the 'snarling,' for there are no headlands at sea!"

"True; I had n't thought of that. But we must certainly see to our own unpacking. It would not do to make our first officers act as our maids."

"*Maids*, Leonora!"

"Stewards, I mean, of course."

But at this moment a splashing was heard alongside, with shrill voices. Dispute was in the air. Discipline was in danger. Is it necessary to say that while the wrangling was still in its green vigor, Mrs. Wester and Mrs. Adair appeared on deck, clad with the majesty of authority, if, in their haste, hatless.

The wind is a lover indeed. He can pay equal attention to two beautiful women at the same moment. Certainly he played with those dark wavy curls and those tangled sunny tresses in the most wantonly bigamic way. There was not one of the crew, from the austere Macfee to Polly the cabin-girl, who did not look with admiration. Truly, skippers to dare death and sea-sickness for !

Is it possible that sea-captains can stop, in the midst of their duties to think of appearances? It may be. Honor, at any rate, looked at Mrs. Wester with delighted eyes. "The sweetest, sunniest, dearest sunbeam of a woman that ever laughed a man's heart away," she murmured to herself. And, indeed, if she was gold within, she was all a-shimmer with the glow without. That hair

99

of hers! As for Leonora, she said nothing then, but under the stars that night she confided to her friend that if she were a man she would go through flood and flame — Mr. Wester had used the phrase once, before their marriage — for that dark loveliness whose name was Honor.

There are people who say that women are never lovers. But — this comes from male arrogance. The male is often only the sauce at the banquet of life, pungent if delectable, obtrusively present if the reverse. It is possible for the flowers and the fruit to admire each other, while admitting the desirability of other stimulants at the feast!

Meanwhile, the crew stared.

"All aboard," exclaimed Captain Adair, with a certain vagueness.

"Aye, aye, mum!"

The crew had spoken with one voice, with the exception of Polly Jones, who had been too shy. When, however, she caught a captainly eye upon her, she blushed purply, and with abrupt shrill anxiety repeated, "Aye, aye, mum!"

The dingey bobbed alongside.

"Trail it astern, O'Leary," said Captain Wester, whereat the red-breasted Bridget moved with alacrity, evidently proud of the confidence placed in her.

This done, Leonora called upon the crew to come aft. She and Honor stood by the compass, whereon a sun-ray danced a joyous farandole. From a paper in her hands she slowly read out the names of those who sailed upon the *Belle Aurore*.

She was about to begin : —

"Men ! "

Then she thought better of it, and thought of "Lasses." But she feared Honor's eyes, the catch in Honor's breath.

"Crew ! " she cried.

"Aye, aye, mum."

"Captain Adair and I wish you all well. After you disperse, First-Officer Moriarty will serve you all a glass of beer to drink good-luck to the *Belle Aurore*."

Here an interruption occurred. Miss Macfee took a step forward.

" Please, mem, Captain Wester, mem, that is *my* department, as I'm the stewardess. Mrs. Moriarty hands tae the food an' the tea, but for mysel, I hae the wines an' speerits in ma charge."

"True, true, Macfee."

A vague regret was in Mrs. Moriarty's eyes, but she restrained herself. If only she had made a stipulation when she had interviewed the ladies in Dublin!—now it was too late.

"And now, eh—ah—*Crew*, I will call over the names."

"Aye, aye, mum,"

"First-Officer—"

At this moment, a whisper warned Leonora not to excite jealousies by giving precedence to either cook or stewardess.

"First-Officers Moriarty and Macfee!"

"Here, mem, if ye plase!"

"Here, mem!"

"First-Officer Macfee, your duties lie mainly aft. Moriarty, you are responsible for the cooking. You are both also to be ready at all times to help in the working of this yacht. There will be two night watches. First-Officer Moriarty will have the first watch, Miss Macfee the second. Captain Adair, will you name the watches?"

Honor swept a searching glance among the crew; a greyhound in pursuit of the flying hare of a smile. It was gone, or it had never been.

"Bridget O'Leary!"

"Here, Capting, I 'm manin', *mum.*"

"Jane Lanigan!"

"Here, if ye please, Capting Miss."

"You two will be in Mrs. Moriarty's watch. Eh — 'm — Mary Murtagh!"

"Yes, your worship!"

"Murtagh, I will trouble you to use no police-court reminiscences."

"No mum, Captings both, beggin' the pardin's av yer honors."

"Polly Jones!"

"Yes, 'm."

"You two will be in Miss Macfee's watch."

Just then a loud noise forward startled every one.

"Drat the baste, it will be afther the crame!" exclaimed First-Officer Moriarty, discipline alone preventing her from an abrupt secession.

"Who is that?" Honor demanded, with a severity that cloaked a hint of alarm.

"Plase, Capting Adair, mem, it's the cat."

"Polly, you go and bring that cat here."

While the cabin-girl pursued the unwilling disturber of the peace, the captains discussed one or two nautical matters, pertinent to the actual commencement of the voyage.

Polly, at last, red and scratched on her round fat hands, returned with a large black cat.

"Whose cat is this?"

There was no answer. Then Miss Macfee spoke.

"It was just found here, mem. He's a stowaway."

"An' if you plase, Captings, 't is for luck the baste is here. A black cat treated well is a good crayture to have in the house — I mane, at say."

"Is that so, Mrs. Moriarty?"

"It is indade, Capting Wester."

"Then he shall be entered on the ship's books. Let me see — We'll call him — we'll call him *Mephisto*."

"Aye, aye, mum."

"Mephisto, your duty will be to look after the mice."

A broad grin came on board, — a grin that developed into a genial all-round laugh when, on Mephisto's being suddenly punched by Polly, a snappy *miaou* came from the latest addition to the yacht's crew.

"And now, my lassies, up with the anchor. Miss Macfee, let go the main-sheet. Captain Adair, will you be so good as to take the wheel? Polly, look alive there, and drop that cat! Take the flag lying yonder and hoist it. Quick, now!"

In a few minutes the anchor was up and made secure. A soft swirl of balmy wind seemed to swim into the deepening hollow of the mainsail. Topsail and jib unfurled like wings. The sea-bird quivered, gently leaned a little to starboard, and glided slowly, then swift and more swift, through the frothing blue water, straight for the sun-dazzle that disclosed the diamond-fields of the sea a mile oceanward.

CHAPTER VI

A FAVORING wind! What magic in the phrase! It is what we all seek, what some of us find without seeking, what we as often as not turn our backs upon.

It meant music to Leonora Wester and to Honor Adair. Every wavelet called laughingly, "All's well!"

What a golden afternoon it was! how lovely the sundown, a vision of straits of pale gold and wide shallows of daffodil, with small clouds like scarlet flamingoes standing indolently on the sunside of purple isles, and over all a sky of such wonderful azure, from harebell blue to the exquisite gray-blue of smoke over woodlands. It was a sun-going to remember.

Two dim shadows lay east and west: Ireland a-lee, the Isle of Man under the white disc floating transparently in the graying blue.

Upon the Irish Channel there were craft bound for every quarter, — luggers, sloops, schooners, brigantines, brigs, ocean-ships, steamers large and small. But, within the range of those on board the *Belle Aurore*, there were few to be seen. Eastward, a yacht's sail flecked a feather in the blue; westward, a brig, full-sailed, stood for the Welsh coast; southward, nothing; northward, a steamer's smoke trailed like an undulating air-serpent.

It was with keen satisfaction Mrs. Wester and Mrs. Adair recognized that their crew was not an *équipage pour rire*. They really knew "the ropes"; not intimately, perhaps, and an emergency might try them, but — well they were efficient, so far. That was good. A passing qualm as to Harry Adair's loyalty had overcome the two adventurers, once the Irish land sank into a purple film. But no, the first shift of the sails proved capacity. As for the helm, each woman at the wheel, of the three who had that post of honor, displayed knowledge, even familiarity.

"We can sleep in peace," Leonora remarked, with a sigh of peace. For the first time since she had left Dublin a thought of her offspring in distant lands had come to her.

Honor pondered.

" Can we, after all, leave the *Belle Au-r're* to the first or second watch? Should we not each take a watch ourselves? Captains generally do. Or they come on deck at intervals. I forget which."

" We can keep ours from eight to twelve — on fine nights. That is, from eight bells to eight bells P. M."

" Oh, Nora dear, there is no such phrase as that. I never heard any one say ' eight bells P. M.' "

" Have *you* crossed from America, Honor ? "

" No, but — "

" My dear, each of us must bring her own store of wisdom to the navigation of this vessel. How are we to know *what* eight bells we mean? I propose that we keep to ' hours.' We can take it as the custom on yachts. If not, it ought to be."

As for Mrs. Moriarty, she proved herself not only a capable first officer, — in so far at least as she did with expedition what she was directed to do, — but an excellent cook. A fault in seawomanship may be forgiven to' one who can turn an omelet with the deftness of a French *cuisinier*. Should not complaisance await the occasional obliviousness of the woman at the wheel who can make coffee as though ordained to that rare and beautiful end?

The *Belle Aurore* seemed to know that she had sailed under a quiet star. The beautiful yawl moved with inimitable grace. Her keel was a transient shadow. The mirrored sails now glided through a silent world; for, with the setting of the sun, the breeze had fallen to a soft breath, and the last white sheep had been driven to its deep-sea fold. The waters lay calm, wonderful in luminous purple, blue, green, or dusky violet, though graying slowly as the twilight sent invisible pioneer shadows to make way for the long summer gloaming.

It is presumable that no captains, or no one who went down to the sea in ships on that day, had a dinner such as was served in this slow-gliding yawl. Impossible to describe that feast, for the viands and the divine draughts that washed them down were

served on plates and in vessels of rainbow-
gold. The fruit came from Eden, the coffee
was of berries grown in the Orient of Heaven,
and the cigarettes witnessed to tobacco plan-
tations amid the groves of Paradise.

This only may be said, on the lower levels;
that Mrs. Moriarty supplied, also, a *purée* of
oysters, two brown sea-savored soles, delicate cutlets from a lamb fresh and sweet as
the green peas it may have glanced at in a
cottage garden, from its sporting-place under
a meadow hawthorn. An omelet there was,
too, foamed at the fringes as the wave that
bore Aphrodité. Dark globes of the grape
held the cooled ardour of sun and earth; a
pine-apple fed the mind with its fragrance, as
well as seduced the two frailest of the senses;
a cluster of Morella cherries lay among some
green leaves, beautiful gypsies there, in that
hot-house company.

And temperate they were, these ladies.
No mixing of fiery wines. Mrs. Wester, a
married woman, a mother, and an American,
took, as a nun might take a benediction, a
tiny anteprandial sip out of a flagon labelled
" Vermouth." There was no other asper-

sion upon the brand of dry champagne, contained in two golden-legended bottles, each but a little laughing pint that knew no harm.

With the coffee, whose compelling fragrance had already wedded the odors of the sea and now longed for union with the quiet flavors of peace lurking in golden Virginia, these joyous captains hesitated. Should they spoil by a breath, a suspicion, that proper pride of the lone, distinctive palate? The question troubled. Cognac — it was old, matured as by grace of God and the care of Bacchic man, conserved flame devoid of any burning fire — obviously expected reverent heed. There was a small flask of Green Chartreuse ; but, well — ladies have been known who would not touch that green loveliness. Leonora said " no," definitely, — a tone familiar to him, desolate in London now, who loved her and called her wife. As for Honor, some reminiscence flaunted a red flag on her cheek. It came and was gone, a fugitive signal. But Mrs. Wester saw it, laughed, and brought a smile, inscrutable certainly, but beautiful, into the

dark eyes of her companion. And so —
the Green Chartreuse was left to its dream of
brown-cowled monks, a sun-splashed monas-
tery, and drowséd memories of the Midi.

Benedictine seduced them. Its delicate
French prose turned the lyric note into an
exquisite common-sense. They rang the
electric bell for Polly Jones.

"Sprite or devil," quoted Mrs. Wester,
reminiscent of Poe, — to the alarm of the
cabin-girl, who stood guiltily agape, till Honor
laughingly bade her close her mouth for fear
a sea-rat might playfully hop into that cav-
ernous cranny.

"Polly, my lass," she added, "we shall
have our coffee and cigarettes on deck."

When they emerged, the moon, fast yel-
lowing, already was weaving its pale gold
through the vast dusky web of the sea. Ju-
piter blazed in the north; south-westward
Venus suspended in a liquid fire. Star after
star came to meet the searching glance.
Night, the night of summer, was come.

CHAPTER VII

N EXT morning Mrs. Wester began a letter to Richard. It was an affectionate epistle, gay too with what seemed to Leonora a fetching irony.

That he did not receive it was not the fault of the post. As a matter of fact, the letter was mentally composed only. But for Honor's enthusiasm it would have been written.

So Richard Wester lost his letter and the sea gained two unexpected Nereids.

For what was this apparition that broke upon Mrs. Wester where she lay in her cosy bunk, her knees tucked up, and a blank sheet of paper outspread for the capture of her marital confidences? Was she still asleep, she wondered? No, for a little ago she had waked, listened with delight to the rippling wash alongside, felt with pleasure the vibration of the yielding planks, and with glee beheld a sunray dancing in at her porthole-window and tickling her lovely (she thought it so, and justly) her lovely, sleepy second-self in the mirror opposite. Then had she not looked at her watch, and found that unconscionable companion fallen into a sea-silence : and had she not lain and wondered if Honor were awake, and then thought of that dutiful letter to Mr. Wester, till a drowsiness — no sleep certainly, merely indolent languor — overcame her, and she had begun to wonder if Mrs. Moriarty and Miss Macfee had declared a deathless feud and were perhaps already far sunk in a cold watery grave ; and if Polly Jones were steering the *Belle Aurore* straight upon a marine forest of reefs set among shallows and quicksands ; and if that was Jacob Macmasters there, menacing, awe-inspiring, with the ruins of the '*Arp o' Hearin* all round him, — with, washing to and fro in the foreground, the drowned bodies, absurd little fat corpses, of poor Bridget O'Leary's twins, with Denis the absent one trying from a rock

to secure one of them with a boat-hook —
and — and — with a start she looked up?
It was Honor.

Honor garbed for the sea!

For a moment Leonora closed her eyes.
Was it possible she had forgotten her bathing
costume, that dainty sea-suit to which she
had given so much delighted thought? If
so, Dublin again: yes, though Harry's Cork-
headland wind might snarl, — aye, even
though her fellow-captain should rage and
imagine a vain thing. Then, in a flash, she
remembered. All was well. She liked hers
better too, for the white braiding and orna-
mentation suited her better than the orange
hue which relieved Honor's, — though, to be
sure, Honor had tied a most seductive
little breast-knot! She could emulate that,
though! While her eyes admired, while her
tongue flattered the vision which had interrupted her, her mind ransacked her scanty
wealth in millinery. A leap at the heart
heralded the conviction that she had a
ribbon made of the very blue of heaven.

Then — O happy Nora — she was kissed.
The vision kissed her! Strange, pleasure

but not rapture met that embrace. Men and women fundamentally the same! Swirling dust!

Reader, male reader, would you or I have been thus insensitive? Think of it, — no, I dare not: nor should you, married or unmarried. In this world many are called, few chosen.

But all that was said was —

"O Honor!"

The next moment Captain Wester was on her feet.

"If not strictly nautical, Nora, you are charming!" This from the rival captain, laughingly.

"Never mind, my dear: if a hero be still a hero in his night-shirt, so may a heroine remain a heroine in her night-gown. But — Honor! — is it *safe* to swim out here, in the open ocean?"

"O you darling donkey, of course it is. We are having a race with a sea-snail somewhere: in other words we crawl. An hour hence we may be becalmed as likely as not. Besides, as we're both such good swimmers, what does it matter whether we have a dip here or within the shore mile? In either case we should be out of our depth!"

"You are always so tiresomely reasonable, Honor! *If* — mind you, I merely hint *if* an accident happened, and we, you or I, eh — ah — *sank* — it would be — ah — so *awkward*, you know, for Richard, or, or, Wilfrid."

"Well, dear, I admit that we could n't expect them to drag for us out *here*."

"O wretched woman — I mean Captain — if you *will* risk our precious lives it must be so. Well, a moment, and I am with you."

The moment extended to several minutes, but at last the white and the orange stood side by side in the cabin.

"I wonder who's on deck" Honor whispered nervously.

"What does it matter? They're only — ah, that is, they're only the crew. Polly Jones may grin, and the crew may giggle: but — well, we'll have our dip!"

"One moment, Nora — Hi, there, Polly! — Polly!"

"Yes 'm! Yes 'm!" came breathlessly

down the cabin stairs, with an immediacy which suggested that Polly had been lying in wait, with ears intent for cabin gossip.

"Polly, tell Miss Macfee to step this way. Ah, never mind — there she is! Good-morning, Miss Macfee!"

"Lord save us, mem, ye're nae gaun on deck wi' thae thin summer-claethin'! It's na the weather for it yet, forbye it's early mornin', an' ye have na had a bite yet."

"Miss Macfee, it isn't customary for lieutenants, or first-officers of any kind, to make remarks on their captain's apparel. However, you sin in ignorance. These are not summer-clothing, but swimming-costumes, and Mrs. — that is, Captain — Wester and I are going in for a swim, as we hope to do every morning, if the weather keeps fine."

"Weel, Captain Adair, mem, and you, mem, ye ken your ain business, but it seems tae me an unco perilous thing tae be jumpin' aff a boat into the deep sea."

"You can stand by, Macfee! Have a rope ready! The moment we sing out 'Lifebelts ahoy!' over you hurl one, two, three!"

Meanwhile Polly had fled. There could be no doubt her errand was the arousing of the crew.

" What if they mutiny? " laughed Leonora.

" And say they cannot permit the suicide of the captains ! "

" Macfee, can you navigate? "

" I hev never tried, Captain Wester, mem, so I canna say."

" Can Mrs. Moriarty? "

Miss Macfee laughed a short, dry, sandy laugh.

" *Navigate !* " she exclaimed; " Mrs. Moriarty ! *Navigate !* "

" Well, well, Macfee, it 's not so unusual to expect a first-officer to know something about navigation. Never mind, I daresay we 're safer without it."

" Besides," Honor broke in, with wise prevision, " you and I, Nora, are familiar with it. So it does not matter."

" True, true ! I had forgotten that, — I mean, I was thinking only of first-officers in general. But come ! This is shivery ! In five seconds my courage will be crying its poor little eyes out in my bed ! " Therewith there was a run, a patter of bare feet, a catching of rapid breath as the keen salt air closed round upon two white necks and four bare arms and two pairs of the comeliest ankles that ever made the heart of a young shoemaker throb. Fortunate breeze ! How the dark and fair tresses waved to and fro, little sprays of blown hair, fluffed, merely fluffed into a bewitching tangle.

The whole crew of the *Belle Aurore* had mustered for the occasion. There was not a hint, a breath of insubordination. An admiration, from professional approval on the part of Mrs. Moriarty — whose sister kept a set of six bathing boxes on Queenstown beach — to adoration blent with awe on the part of Polly Jones, exhibited itself.

Two glances swept the horizon. There were no vessels near. Far off, all save northward, were divers craft, chiefly coasters and small sloops. Not a steamer even, and, above all, no neighboring yacht. Then the searching eyes had time to look at the beauty of that glorious morning. The sun swept the waves as with a gigantic golden scythe. The splendor of the sun scattered silver everywhere with superb profusion. A universal rippling and dappling into little hollows showed that the breeze had not wakened a single white-sheep; though now and then a mere lambkin of foam frisked a dazzling patch of white fleece, and then scurried off down this or that green lawn to this or that blue fold.

Never was there a more seductive sea. Every violet patch, every azure reach, every purplish strait was alive with sunfire. Beneath the yacht, a deep lustrous green shelved into emerald.

"Now, Nora, now; O glory!" cried Honor joyously, as with a run she cleared the yard or two of deck, just alighted on the port gangway, which Polly or some other ministering angel had lowered, and with a leap was in the water, head-foremost, cleancut as a sea-mew, a seal, a diving otter, a mermaid from a rock!

"*Ah — h — h !*"

That inarticulate gurgle was — *music*. Perhaps no one there called it so; but many a song-burst dies unheard. That sounds as though some poet had said it; so runs the rhythm; well, singer unknown, pardon!

Music! So any one, — any male, who might have heard it, would have said.

It came from Captain Wester.

It was the safety-valve of stifled rapture.

The next moment there was another blue shadow aflit across the deck; another leaping Nereid; another splash.

The sea held the two captains. All discipline was at an end. The cabin-girl was wedged in between the two first-officers, and Bridget O'Leary's ample bust inclined like an impendent avalanche over the shoulder of Miss Macfee. Nay, more, the clutch of Jane Lanigan's fist upon the soft side of the Moriarty muscles was unnoticed till a sudden tautening produced a most unmatronly curse.

"Ah shure, the darlints," said Bridget the indiscreet, admiringly, — "just look at thim, Mary! Faith, they're like ducks bhobbin' up an' down in the blue wather there!"

"Whist, ye blatherskite!"

"Ah, saints in hiven, did ye ever see the loike o' *that*, now?"

"Whoop! There they go, — shure it's amazin' how they don't sink, an' it's so deep too!"

" Well, well, 't is eddycation does it.   An'
it's that that Pathrick and Phelim 'll have,
bless me pore bhoys, — ah, and it's God
knows what thim childher are doin' now !
Jane Lanigan, take your slop-bucket of a
fhist out o' my side ! "

" They 're comin' !   They 're comin' ! "

" Back there !   Ye aggravatin' ignyrant
craytures, d' ye know what ud happen if
there wis anny wind at all at all !   Why, it's
taken aback we 'd be !   An' not a soul at
the wheel !   Holy Virgin, 't is enough to
make a cat swear !   Mary Murtagh, you go
to that wheel quicker than you can wink,
or I 'll know the rayson why !   You there,
Lanigan, haul in that rope, — no !   no !
Jasus Christ av pity on you, woman !   't is
the topsail rope I 'm manin' !   Polly Jones,
you hurry up with thim towels for the Captings, or it's the worst skelping you 've ever
had you 'll be getting ! "

Mrs. Moriarty had a voice.   Of that there
could be no question.   Its stentorian boom
was like a thump upon the backs of those to
whom she addressed herself.

Honor and Leonora heard it too, amid the

lapping of the water and the splash of the wavelets against the white rows of their breasts and under their sweeping arms. Their laughter rippled.

Ah, the delight of that morning swim ! the exquisite rhythmic motion ; the buoyancy of the salt sea ; the feeling as though the water was electrified by the sun, and every inch of the body bathed in fluid gold ; the soft, swift yielding, the swifter inflow and embrace ; the rippling past ear and neck of the running wave ; the sight, the smell, the wonder, the intoxication !

Panting, the swimmers drew near.

"Look, Honor," Leonora gasped, baffling an eddy that tried to leap down her throat, "is n't she lovely ! "

As, at that moment, the round red countenance of Mrs. Moriarty was looming over the taffrail, Honor thought the exclamation was intended for the co-first-officer, instead of the *Belle Aurore.* The temptation to avenge herself upon her too quizzical comrade was more than she could withstand.

With a lurch she seized Captain Wester's left foot, just as that officer was about to lift herself out of the water by the rope dangling alongside the port-gangway.

Splutter, splash, and a stifled yell! Ignominiously, a commander sank, screeching.

"*Kismet!*" cried Honor, while, poised for a second on the lowest step, she let the brine stream from her; then, with a joyous laugh, when she saw a golden head emerge from the deep as though propelled from a catapult, she clambered aboard, left a dripping trail upon the white deck, and disappeared into the happy haven of her cabin.

CHAPTER VIII

WHEN Leonora came on deck, she saw the need for authority. The grin extended from Macfee to Polly Jones.

A glance sufficed.

The mainsail had been furled. The yacht might as well have been in Dublin Bay all night. Had she been laying-to all night? The thought was a humiliating one.

But Captain Wester had not coached herself for nothing.

" Cast off these tyers, there ; slack out the main sheet ! Now, then, Lanigan, and you, Murtagh, hoist the peak and belay the peak halyards, — and see you coil the halyards neatly close under their cleats."

How she hoped Honor was listening ! Had Captain Adair any idea that her colleague was so apt in sea-talk ? Ah, the secret of that ! — but no.

Her alacrity of phrase, even more than her commanding tone, had a marked effect. Bustle prevailed. Mrs. Moriarty gave a hasty glance to see that the coffee was not boiling over, and then spanked Polly Jones's ears for not coiling a halyard lying under her very nose.

"Now, then, Miss Macfee, don't let the crew coil halyards in that lubberly way. Capsize them, — capsize them!"

But here a whispered voice came from the cabin stairs. None heard it except Captain Wester, unless it was Bridget O'Leary, who was at the wheel, though with a face innocent of delight. "Nora darling, are you out of your mind? Do come down!"

Almost it seemed as if the crew entertained some such idea also.

"Capsize them!"

What did it mean? Was it a nautical term, or a threat? If it had been 'capsize her' the allusion might have been to Polly, who was snivelling, or to Lanigan, who had caught her ankle in a coil and was palliating her wrath by painful Cork expletives.

"Don't you know how to capsize, you

lubbers! Turn the halyards over, so that the end is under the coil!"

All hoped that Captain Wester would now go below. She was dripping, and probably catching cold. It was not solicitude for her, however.

" Why is that jib down, Miss Macfee?"

" Well, mem, I dinna just ken."

" Be so good as to ken in future. This yacht is not a canal-barge. You there, have the bobstay and bowsprit shrouds been hove taut?"

" Aye, aye, mum!"

" Well, haul out the tack on the traveller — belay the outhaul — look out, there, keep the jib out of the water — hoist the halyards taut, and belay! You, Lanigan and Murtagh, trim in the lee sheet. Now, then, stand by to tend the jib and foresheets. Are you ready, O'Leary?"

A nod came from the attentive Bridget, apoplectic with excitement.

" Then *Ready about!*"

There was a moment of breathless silence. Then O'Leary sang out *Helm's-a-lee*, and brought the yawl up into the wind, such as there was, as though she were a skilled driver with a sensitive horse.

But it was just a trifle overdone. The fitful breeze wandering by saw this and gleefully took advantage. The *Belle Aurore* suddenly lay up in the wind, her sails shaking.

"What's the matter, Nora? For Heaven's sake let us go either forward or backward, but not shiver here in this ridiculous fashion!"

Was it anger or fear that palpitated in Honor's usually sweet voice? It was shrill, alas. Captain Wester's nerves felt the blight.

"Avast!" she exclaimed, — with undue emphasis, Honor thought a sneering severity.

"I will not avast, Leonora," replied the reprimanded. "Don't you know what you have done? You have caused the yacht to miss stays and get in irons."

Mrs. Wester stared.

Could this be Honor Adair? *She* had picked up a store of marine knowledge, but had Honor *dreamed* herself into knowledge? It was incredible. And yet — no, of a certainty Mrs. Adair would never have made that allusion to stays if she had not been sure of what she was saying. However, it was not a time to bandy words. The yawl had now lost headway.

"Haul the head sheets to windward," she cried, a little quaveringly because of the chill that was now upon her.

"O'Leary, put the helm to starboard. You there, slack out the main and mizzen sheets ! "

The vessel now began to move slowly on the port tack.

"Miss Macfee ! "

"Yes, mem."

"When she has paid off sufficiently, trim the sheets. Keep her on the port tack."

With that, Leonora gave a final glance that embraced the yacht, the sails, the sea around, and the heaven above : and, with as much dignity as was possible in the circumstances went below.

The moment she had disappeared the crew looked at each other.

"Weel, guid sakes ! " muttered First-Officer Macfee, below her breath.

First-Officer Moriarty was more explicit.

"Well gyurls, I'm damned — by all the Sints I'm damned — if the loike o' that was iver seen afore! Talk o' men! Why, there isn't a capting on the say knows more than *she* does!"

"An' her in costoom too, an' dhrippin' wet," murmured Jane Lanigan.

"The knowledge av 'er!" Mary Murtagh could ejaculate no more than this.

More might have been said, but a shrill screech from Polly Jones testified to the fact that the coffee was boiling over.

Meanwhile the two captains stood facing each other in the cabin. Captain Wester dripped *in statu quo*. Captain Adair was wrapped in a huge bath-towel. Both looked so fresh and lovely, so cool and sweet and exquisitely well, that no imp of discord could have remained for more than a second.

"O Nora, you darling, wise, extraordinary, ridiculous, delightful dear!"

"Why, Honor, what *are* you after?"

"After! It's *you*, mavourneen!"

"Oh, I was only giving a few words to the crew. They need looking after."

"Captain darlint, if you 'll allow me I 'll have that towel, for I 'm flooding the cabin, to say nothing of laying the foundation of a rapid consumption."

A scuffle, a ripple of laughter, and Honor retreated victorious.

Wet and happy, Mrs. Wester sought her own cabin. The two called to each other in joyous badinage while they dressed, and Polly Jones set the breakfast. Soon that eagerly desired meal made its appearance tended by Miss Macfee.

There were not such rolls, such butter and cream, such bacon and eggs, such grilled kidneys, such marmalade, such coffee, such a white cloth, such a bowl of roses, on any other table, on sea or land !

It was done justice to, that meal.

"After all, Honor," said Mrs. Wester, near the end, peeling a mandarin orange : " after all, you too know more than I thought you did. That remark about the stays was learned in no milliner's establishment ! "

Honor laughed a slight flush on her bonny face.

" I do happen to know a few things about

sailing. Of course, dear, I have n't *your* thorough knowledge."

" H'm — can you — eh — ah — scandalize a mainsail? "

Was this a trap, Honor wondered. It was impossible to guess from Leonora's face. Demureness dwelled there. On the whole the chances were that Mrs. Wester was taking her revenge. Still, marine phraseology abounded in incongruities and idiocies, and it was possible that mainsails *could* be scandalized. She would compromise.

"What did you say, dear? I did not quite catch it."

" I asked, my dear Captain Adair," Leonora answered dryly, " I asked, can you scandalize a mainsail? "

" I am surprised, Nora, that one of so exact a mind as yours, and trained too by so strict a business man as Richard, should not be more explicit. Now of course *I* know what you mean : but a stranger would hardly understood whether by '*can you,*' you meant ' are you able to,' or ' is such a thing possible '? "

A shout of laughter filled the cabin with music.

Polly Jones appeared prompt as a pantomime imp.

" Yes, 'm ! "

" Polly, bring me the log-book; there it is, on the bunker yonder. Thanks; that will do. Be off with you, and come down and let us know the moment the wind freshens or veers. And now, Honor, excuse me a moment. I *must* record the extraordinary effect of the sea upon you."

" Why, what do you mean, you dear madcap ? "

Mrs. Wester wrote rapidly with a pencil, and then, holding the book to one side with a critical air, read aloud : —

" *Strange Incarnation of the G. O. M. at sea.*"

"In reply to a simple question, the generally direct and simple Captain Honor Adair spoke so much in the manner and after the method of Mr. W——m E——t G——e (*this is delicately hinted, I think*) that there can be no question as to her having been *pro tem.* an actual incarnation of that mysterious and occult being, the G. O. M. This comes strangely home to us, after our recent scepticism at an Esoteric Buddhist's house, where we had coffee and psychology, morning dress at 8 P.M., and a drear company of frumps and male frights.

"I shall watch further developments with interest, if not without anxiety, and shall communicate the results to the Psychical Research Society."

"Oh, you golden-haired, darling atrocity! I warn you, I'll be even with you for that! Apologize — withdraw — or, or, I'll, I'll — "

"What?"

"Scandalize you as well as the mainsail!"

"Ha, ha, Capting, my Capting! Now I have you! Tell me straight, *can you scandalize the mainsail?*"

"Yes, Nora, I can."

"You can? Well, then, how?"

"By compromising its relations with the flying jib."

For a moment Mrs. Wester was nonplussed. There was an air of assurance in her colleague's voice. Then it flashed upon her.

"Oh, you fraud, you fraud! How dare you, Honor, impute evil ways and doings to those innocent white sails! I ask you, you scaramouch, how dare you?"

"Well, dear, you would insist on my scandalizing that mainsail somehow or other. and I could n't see any way out of it except by implicating that respectable party in a *liaison* with another sail!"

"You are a nice person to go to sea in a yacht! Now tell me, Honor dear, are n't you glad, are n't you just a little relieved to find that you are with some one who knows so much about sailing?"

"Indeed, I am, Nora."

"Yes, but you don't look it. You are laughing behind your eyes!"

"Laughing, darling? Oh, no, no, Leonora Wester, I am not laughing."

"Then what is it you are after?"

"How dear old Ireland survives through the veneer of American civilization! Only, Captain Wester, you should say phwat am I afther, me bhoy!"

"Me gurl, you mane, Kathy acushla! But look here now, Honor, admit you are surprised, and that you had no idea I knew so much ! ''

"Indeed, indeed, I am surprised. But I am glad, very glad. For I want to learn. It is so easy to scandalize one's friends and relations, but who of us can scandalize a mainsail without previous knowledge of marine ethics ! No, dear, far from mocking, I am eager to learn from you See here ! '' —

— As she spoke, Honor withdrew from a side pocket a slip of paper containing several pencilled memoranda.

"What's this, dear?" There was a certain solicitousness in Captain Wester's voice which did not escape her colleague.

"Oh, nothing that you won't be able to answer straightaway. But first they are mere nothings, that I daresay Polly Jones knows. I am so ashamed of my ignorance. What puzzles me is the different meanings yachtsmen attach to words which we landlubbers (and by 'we' I don't mean *you*, of course, dear Leonora) use in the ordinary way. Now, what is an *earring*, a *guy*, a *bridle*, a *bumpkin*, a *garboard streak*, a *cringle*, a

thimble, a *crutch*, a *toggle*, a *tabernacle ;*
what are *water-ways, limbers, hounds, coam-
ings, channels, battens,* and *gimbals ;* what is
the meaning of to *brail* and to *bream*, to
chock a block, to *guy a mainboom*, to *house*,
to *mouse*, to *sag*, and to *jibe ?* "

Mrs. Wester had grown paler as this cate-
gory proceeded. Often she had heard Richard allude to " a dark horse." Was Honor
a — a — mare of that particular breed ?

She pulled herself together. Tabernacle
and thimbles, bridles and earrings, these at
least were inventions of captainly malice and
jealousy.

" My dear, I do not think you need ask
me the meaning of that last term. To *jibe*
is as easy to do on a yacht as on land ; at
least so it seems to me, my dear Mrs. Adair."

Honor remained unmoved.

" However," she resumed, " these little
matters you can explain to me at your leisure.
What I *should* like to know at once, in case
— eh — ah — the weather should change
suddenly — and we ought to be prepared,
of course, for every emergency — is as follows : very ordinary questions they will seem

to *you.* — First, then : what is the actual difference between 'bear away' and 'bear up'? Again, what between 'put the helm up' and 'put the helm down'? H'm !"

" I will hear you out, Honor, before I reply."

" Very good. How would you advise me to proceed in order to find the area of the jib-header, of the spinnaker, and other head sails ? "

" Go on, Honor, I am listening."

" I am still puzzled about sails. In the case of a yawl having a lug mizzen, what would be taken as the upper boundaries ? "

Almost did Honor's heart relent. Could these be tears, the bitter dew of chagrin, coming into Captain Wester's blue eyes?

She looked away. Then, slowly, she withdrew another slip of paper from her jacket pocket.

" Just glance at this, Nora, like a dear."

" What is it ? "

" Don't look at it so fearfully ! It won't bite ! "

" But what is it ? What are these horrid figures about ? "

"It is this : —

"Supposing a vessel's rating is x, t, the allowance she makes per knot to a yacht whose rating is 1, will be thus found: $t = 360 \dfrac{-360}{5\sqrt{x}}$. The result is the allowance in seconds. As the allowance is calculated for one knot, the allowance for another distance will be found by multiplying t by the length of the course in knots. To calculate the allowance that should be made by one yacht to another, find the t, as above, for both yachts; subtract the lesser from the greater t. — And now, Nora, I solemnly ask you, what does all this mean, and what happens when you *have* subtracted all the tea-leaves from the *tea*, — no, I mean the lesser from the greater t ? "

A sob, faint but audible, broke upon Honor's ear.

Captain Wester had been beaten on her own ground, or, to be more apt, on her own water.

"Oh Honor, Honor, it is n't fair ! It is n't, it is n't ! "

" What is n't, Nora darling ? "

"O don't call me darling! I hate the word. A silly synonym for little goose, that is what it is!"

"But — darling — "

"There you go again, Honor Adair! Have n't I just told you that darling is the same as goose, — as *goose*, I tell you!"

"I never heard it taken in that way, Leonora."

"Honor, sometimes you can be positively *hateful!* Why do you call me Leonora, as formally as though you wore a white choker and were acting as the clergyman at my christening!"

"Well, dear, because it is your name. But I can call you Mrs. Wester!"

"You know you dare not, except in fun."

"Well, Captain Wester, then."

"No, not just now; it is too formal."

"O well, then, Wester simply."

"I wish Wilfrid were here just now, *He* would n't smile as you are doing just now. He —"

"No; I know what he would be saying."

"What?"

"He would be turning to Richard, and

saying : 'Confound it, Dick, what *are* these two donkeys squabbling about ! ' "

At this Captain Wester turned a flushed eager face to Captain Adair. A rainbow gleam was in her eyes. Hope made her a girl again. Reconciliation was imminent.

" Honor," she said in little more than a whisper, " what would Richard say to that ? "

" Dearest, he would say in his dry way : " ' Let 'em be, Wilf. Don't you know they are lovers, and that this is only a lover's tiff ? The only real cause of dispute between them is, that they can't make up their minds as to who loves the other best ! ' "

" Bad grammar, Honor acushla, but O I am so glad ! *We* must n't quarrel, dear ; we, of all people in the world."

" That we won't ! Not that I ever meant to, you sweetest provokingest donkey that ever was ! Only I knew what you were up to — so I coached too, Captain Wester — and, and, it is thinking I am that I know just about as much and just about as little as my dear and worthy Colleague ! And now we 'll drop, once and for all, all that silly jargon ! "

"Voted *nem. con!* Passed in Supply! Decree *nisi!*"

"O you heavenly silly Honor, let me kiss you."

"I will. I am not proud, nay nor miserly."

"Bah! Take that — and that — and that!"

"One word, dear, before we go on deck!"

"Yes?"

"May I — may I — call you — eh — a little goose?"

"Yes, darling!"

CHAPTER IX

SO came and went the only fresh breeze of that morning.

The wind, which had freshened for a moment, died away. An exquisite sapphire noon was slowly wrought out of the blue and gold. There was just breath enough to move the *Belle Aurore*, or perhaps it was mainly the current that gave movement enough to allow the helm purchase.

A deep content fell upon all. Forward, Polly Jones slept upon a coil of rope, into which she had sunk and whence only her head and one shoulder emerged. The effect was that of a cobra in a profound snooze.

The crew except Mary Murtagh, who dozed at the idle wheel, lay here and there, too lazy and too comfortable even to talk. First-Officer Moriarty sat on the deck with her back to the mast, a black cutty pipe in her mouth, and the peace that passeth understanding upon her face.

Now and again, she indulged in a monologue, or addressed a casual remark to Miss Macfee or to O'Leary.

" Yiss," she murmured sleepily, " 't is a cruel onsartain world at the best o' times."

The remark was apposite to a confidence from Bridget concerning Denis and Phelim.

" That 's the wurrd, Mrs. Moriarty. You are a woman of the wurrld, indade, an' no mhistake. Onsartain ; that 's what it is, an' that 's what I sed when thim twins came. Who 's to know that two pair o' little shoes is wanted instead o' wan pair only, as is usual in the way o' life ! "

" It 's right you are, Bridget. There 's no knowin' how thim things is managed. It 's just this, as me ould mother, the Sints keep her, used to say ; if you want thim, you can't get thim ; an' if you don't want thim, shure an' they 'll come at the wrong time, or like two loaves whin you know you han't the change to pay comfortable for wan."

A deep sigh followed. Silence reigned everywhere, save for the faint wash of the water to windward, and the indeterminate whispering sound that the sea utters with its innumerous hushed lips, even in the sleep of a dead calm.

Miss Macfee sat bolt upright, with her back against the starboard side of the mast. In her lap was a Bible. Her angular face was softened as she gazed into the blue stillness northward. Perhaps she heard in her mind the bells of Greenock summoning the good folk to the kirk.

Her colleague glanced at her. A genial soul she was, this Moriarty, and though a Protestant seemed to her a pig without a tail, she was not one to deny that good bacon might be saved and cured out of such unpromising material.

"Miss Macfee, would ye be carin' to read us somethin' out o' the Bible ye have there?"

"Weel, Mrs. Moriarty, I hev the Book here, for it's the Sawbath-day; and yachts or no yachts, swims or no swims, smokin' an' idlin' or not, it's ma pleesure an' ma duty to see to ma speeritual welfare."

"An' quite right, too, Miss Macfee. But

as it's the Holy Day, an' as no wan here is particular, I'm shure it wud be a pleasure to hear ye read us a bit. As for that innycent craytur, Polly Jones, shure it won't hurt her, and she aslape there, just like my ould tom-cat in Cork, sound as punch till ye'd be for sayin' *milk*."

"It's na my place, Mrs. Moriarty. I ken my place, though my immortal soul is my ain."

"But what thin?"

"It's a sair grief tae me that there's sae muckle levity aboard this yacht, an' on the Sawbath-day. I had hopit there would be prayers, as on all ships that gae doon to the sea."

"Shure an' it's aisy to ask the ladies. Jist you go and say that to thim, Miss Macfee."

"Say *whet*, Mrs. Moriarty?"

"That it's wantin' to kape the Sabbath-day holy ye are."

"Hoots, mem, they're probably Papist bodies like yersel."

"Swate crayturs, both av thim."

"An' forby that, it's no inclined I am to

share the blessing wi' them as willna tak to it by grace from within."

This gave subject for thought.

Mrs. Moriarty sucked at her cutty. The blue wreaths of smoke ascended like incense from that pondering brain. "I 'm for tellin' ye phwat I think, Miss Macfee," she said at last, in a slow impressive voice, and with her gaze corkscrewing the indolent mind of Bridget, who cared more to talk about the twins, than about any religious problem that could possibly occur.

"Weel, mem?"

"Thim blessins that are meant for the few are jist puff-tarts. They look onticin' in the pasthry-cook's windy, but when ye 've had 'em an' it's all over ye 're jist where ye was. An phwat 's more; thim swates are apt to turn the stummick, ye get so fond o' your puff-tarts that ye say there 's nothin' else goin' that is worth havin'. An' all the toime we 're just as happy, an' are feedin' up in our own way. Shure enough, wumman, we all get to the praste and the sexton an' the wake an' the ghlory whether we ate puff-tarts or onpretentious praties!"

"Aye, Mrs. Moriarty. I ken weel what ye mean. But it's a puir dementit mind ye have if ye think ye'll get to what in yer heathen papistical way ye call the glory, except by faith."

"Faith now, here's a divarsion at last. By the sowl o' my uncle Tim the fiddler, — God rest 'im, an' a good man he was, for all he died from makin' love too long to the whiskey bottle, — it's music we're goin' to have!"

Miss Macfee turned her head. After all, perhaps the Captains were godly folk.

Alas, it was a guitar.

Captain Wester was the culprit.

It was evident that a Sunday service was not intended. Miss Macfee sorrowed, but in her heart of hearts was a certain curiosity. She had never heard a guitar played, and knew the instrument only by repute. The Rev. Peter Macfee, her cousin at Greenock, had spoken of it once as an ungodly thing, attuned to Babylonish music.

When the first few notes came humming along the deck, there was a glad movement, a stir of expectation, among the listeners.

Wives in Exile

With a start, Polly Jones awoke, stumbled to her feet, and cried shrilly, " *Yes'm!* "

" Sit down, ye ongainly frog," said Mrs. Moriarty, severely, as she knocked the ashes out of her pipe, and prepared to relight, on her face an expression of sheer content.

On a low deck-chair Leonora reclined, the guitar in her lap, and just responsive to her slight wandering touches. Honor lay on a soft bear-skin rug, her hands claspt behind her back and her beautiful eyes fixt upon the abysses of that deep vault wherein the other stars were invisible.

It was as though the sea's thoughts were moving into music. Leonora played the guitar as though it were her voice and she a born singer. Her touch vivified. When, at last, she broke into a wild plantation melody, there was a hush on board.

Then, abruptly, she passed into a gay little Spanish dance, wherein the twinkling feet of the dancers were audible, and light laughter, and rhythmic movement.

"And now, Honor, you must sing," she whispered, as she struck the last notes of an old Irish melody.

"I don't know what to sing, Nora. Besides, I am too lazy."

"Nonsense. Sing that song of your own, the one Wilfrid is so fond of. See, here is the air for it."

Whenever Honor sang, those who did not know her were always taken by surprise. In her voice was a poignant sweetness, a haunting beauty that, as Leonora used to declare jokingly, was as good as having a large bank-account in reserve, for, as she would add, "Honor's voice is made up of notes payable in gold."

Rising till she supported herself on her right elbow, she began her song; soft and low at first, but swelling into a wonderfully full and rich contralto.

"O Day, come unto me,
    Fair and so sweet!
Crown'd shalt thou be,
    And with wing'd feet
Escape the invading sea,
    Whose bitter line
    Follows o'er fleet.
What joy thou would'st is thine:
Life is divine,
    O Fair and Sweet!

"Death is a paltry thought:
　　A little troublous thing —
　　An insect's sting!
　Beautiful Day, oh, heed it not !
　Surely I hear the rumor of thy feet,
　　And Death is vain — draw near, draw near ! —
　Alas, and is it so?　Farewell, O Fair and Sweet,
　　For Death is here."

Not a sound was heard as she finished. She knew well, however, that every one on board was bewitched. It was not for want of experience that she knew how she could win silence and tears with any company.

"Honor, dear, sing that song of the Roses. It was *born* for a guitar. I know just the air for it. Here . . . is not that right? *Do* sing it."

With a wonderful high sweet lilt, like a mounting bird, the sweet voice soared above the sunlit water with the sunswept ocean-air.

"Roses, roses,
　Yellow and red ;
　A rose for the living,
　A rose for the dead !
　Who 'll sip their dew ?
　There are only a few
　Of the yellow and red ;
　Youth sells its roses
　Ere youth is sped.

Wives in Exile

"Roses, roses,
All for delight;
What of the night?
Hark, the tramp, tramp,
The scabbard's clamp,
The flaring lamp!
Where is the morning dew?
Ah, only a few
Drank ere the yellow and red
Lay shrivelled, shrivelled,
Over the dead.

"Roses, roses,
Buy, oh, buy!
The years fly,
'T is the time of roses.
Here are posies
For one and all,
For lovers that sigh
And for lovers that die;
And for love's pall
And burial!

"Roses, roses, roses, buy, buy, oh, buy!
Why delay, why delay, roses also die.

"Pink and yellow, blood-red, snow-white:
Roses for dayspring, roses for night!

"Buy, buy, oh, my roses buy!
A kiss for a kiss, and a sigh for a sigh!"

It was quite impossible for discipline to withstand this shower of roses.

A loud round of clapping came from the foredeck.

Captain Wester glanced forward, and, with a smile, nodded appreciatively. As for Honor, she gave a pleased little laugh and sank back on her bearskin.

A whispered consultation was evidently going on forward.

" I wonder what they 're up to," murmured Leonora, low, so that Murtagh should not overhear. " I expect they want something more. After all, it 's their holiday, too, poor things. And then, it 's Sunday, and as we 're having no prayers, we might —

" Oh, you special pleader ! But you give them a negro melody, or one of your Spanish songs. They will like that better, unless our friend Macfee thinks them too ungodly for the Sabbath."

"Ah, I forgot all about dear old Macfee. Honor, you could n't rise to a hymn could you ? Surely there 's something — ' How beautiful upon the mountains,' or something or other — that would fit into the ' Wearin' o' the Green.' I 'm sure *that* would do nicely."

At that moment Polly came aft slowly. When close to Mrs. Wester, she stopped, blushed, and inarticulately murmured.

"Please 'm," !

"Yes, Polly?"

"Please 'm, Capt'n 'm ! Mrs. Moriarty an' the rest av us, I mane av the crew, would be takin' it kindly if you an' Mrs. Captain Adair would be givin' us some more music an' singin'."

"What does Miss Macfee say?"

"Shure, please 'm, she 's ready to hould on."

"To hold on? Oh, very well : that 's very kind of her indeed."

"An' please 'm, she said if there was a hymn goin' she 'd be plased indade, not manin' any liberty, but hopin' it might be so. An' Mrs. Moriarty, 'm, she 'oped it might be a ballad, she did : for her uncle Tim, she sed, was that fond o' ballads, an' her heart melts, an' she loves the guitar the best o' all the instrymints afther the fiddle."

"And Lanigan? And O'Leary? And — eh — and Polly?"

A deeper blush than ever swept over the dear dimpling face.

"Oh, indade, 'm, it's not for the likes o' us to say."

"Well, go back and say that we have n't any hymns, but we 'll do the best we can with another song or two."

"Honor!"

"Yes?"

"*Do* give them that song you sang and shocked the Reverend James with one Sunday evening, when he thought you were going to sing an anthem!"

"Which one? Oh, yes, I know; 'Tim Ryan!' Well, here goes. Play the air of 'The Pigs of Ballyshannon.'"

And with that Captain Adair, with a deep rich brogue and long drawl or short catch, accompanied the thrumming of the guitar, —

> "Ah, sure my heart is
> Set on Tim Ryan!
> Oh, if only he knew
> I was dyin'!
> Dyin' for love o' him,
> Ongrateful, hard-hearted,
> Who cares not a pin
> That we 're severed an' parted!

"'Tis a curse on the men,
It's little they need us!
If we sob they grow deaf,
Though laugh an' they'll heed us!
Oh, Tim Ryan,
Is it blind you be
Not to know I'm dyin'
For love o' thee?

"Oh, acushla, asthore,
Dear Tim, is that you now?
I thought 't was the hen
Or Peggy the cow!
Sure is that true
That 't is *you* that's dyin'
An' all for to make me
Mrs. Tim Ryan?

"Oh, faith, thin, be aisy!
There's time an' to spare!
Lave off, now, Tim,
Lave smoothin' my hair!
Oh, well, yes, 't is laughin'
I was with my dyin' —
Still, I'm thinkin' I'll be
Mrs. Ryan!"

Delight greeted this song. Miss Macfee remained unmoved, or moved only to silent regret. Surely the Sabbath was made for other matters than the courtin' of Tim Ryan!

"Oh, do give us one more song, Honor dear! It's too lovely to lie here in this glorious sunshine and sweet air, — just to lie and hear you sing."

"Let it be one, then. And a sad one, after the happiness of Mr. and Mrs. Tim Ryan!"

The song that Honor sang now was to a low and wailing air, sad as twilight at sea.

"The moonwhite waters wash and leap,
    The dark tide floods the Coves of Crail;
Sound, sound he lies in dreamless sleep,
    Nor hears the sea-wind wail.

"The pale gold of his oozy locks
    Doth hither drift and thither wave;
His thin hands plash against the rocks,
    His white lips nothing crave.

"Afar away she laughs and sings
    A song he loved, a wild sea-strain, —
Of how the mermen weave their rings
    Upon the reef-set main.

"Sound, sound he lies in dreamless sleep,
    Nor hears the sea-wind wail,
Though with the tide his white hands creep
    Amid the Coves of Crail."

After that there was silence again. In the noon-heat, Mary Murtagh drowsed at the wheel; the crew slumbered, save First-Officer Macfee, who read diligently. Honor dreamed, with sleepy eyes watching the vibrations of light in the blue sky. A soft low snore came, intermittently, from Captain Wester.

CHAPTER X

EIGHT bells !
Noon ! Was it noon already?
Golden hours, shod with silence, how they
slip by almost unnoted, unheard.

" If you plase, mum ! "

The voice was that of Mrs. Moriarty.

" If you plase, Capt'n Adair."

" Yes, Moriarty ? "

" There 's a shaddy comin' up out o' the
south. I 've seen the same too often, whin
I was aboard that Calcutty boat I sailed in
as stewardess, before I met Moriarty. It 's
in the Chiney say I 'm manin.' "

" What 's the shadow doing there ? "

" It 's not what it 's doin' there, Mrs.
Adair, mum, — Capting, I should say, — but
what it will be manin' to do *here*."

" Do you think it means a change ? "

" I do, an' a bad wan at that."

" H'm, — Mrs. Moriarty, is luncheon nearly
ready? In half an hour you say? Well, let
us have it as soon as you can. We may as
well have it first, and tackle that shadow
afterwards."

" Nora, do you hear that about the
shadow?"

" I do, but it's probably only a passing
thunder-cloud. The glass is right enough."

" I expect we'll have a breeze all the
same, — a stiff one, I mean. Moriarty
really knows a good deal, and I could see
she thinks we are going to have a change."

" Well, Honor, you have done the very
best thing you could; namely, to order
luncheon, and leave the shadow alone, meanwhile."

But the shadow — as shadows will at sea
— did not care to be left to itself.

While the two captains lingered over their
coffee and fruit, it widened and darkened,
and crept rapidly northward. Its dusky
feet were stealthily approaching the *Belle
Aurore*.

" Hark !" exclaimed Mrs. Wester, suddenly. " Do you hear that, Honor ?" It

was a soughing wail o' the wind, low but ominous.

"Yes. And there's rain in that, too. We'd better put on our pilot-coats."

The precaution was advisable. When they came on deck, the whole scene had changed.

The sea was still quite calm, but the blue had gone out of it. Wherever it was not of a slaty hue, it was green, in places vividly green. Here and there patches of a livid color were interspersed.

The air, too, had suddenly grown still, — damp with the breath of coming rain. Out of the white glare in the south, long films of almost impalpable mist extended across the sky. The further ends of these were serrated and fringed.

"It's a thunder-burst, I think, Honor," said Leonora uneasily, as she moved restlessly up and down the deck, looking now at the compass, now at the flapping sails.

"I expect it's more than that. Look at the edges of that whiteness down there in the southwest. I daresay Moriarty's right. Besides, the glass is now falling steadily. It has been falling since the forenoon, I 've just discovered; the reason why I thought it was steady was because the signal-hand had been moved by Polly Jones."

" Well, there 's one consolation; the wind will take us on a right tack. Do you know — Honor — "

" What?"

" Well, do you know, it 's a little foolish of us not to have waited for a really good breeze, — one that would have taken us over to the Scottish coast in no time."

" Oh, we 'll be there soon enough. We ought to sight Ailsa Craig this evening, — sooner, if a heavy spurt of wind comes on."

" H'm, I hope we won't sight it in a driving squall, and just ahead of us!"

" Thank goodness, dear, both Moriarty and Macfee are trustworthy enough. For all their ignorance of some matters, they have both been to sea a good deal, and as Harry assured us, really do know something about sailing small craft. And then, — well, they don't suffer from seasickness."

" But you don't either, you told me, Honor?"

" N — n — no. Nor you? "

" Oh, no."

But even as they chatted, the imminent squall came nearer and nearer. A faint humming sound could be heard away in the southwest. The horizon seemed to have lifted itself into a dark line. This line constantly spilled over in a thin wavy whiteness. As Honor and Leonora watched, they could see this white lip moving nearer.

Mrs. Moriarty came up, touching her felt cap.

" She 's a good boat, the *Bell Hooroar*, Capting Wester, mum, an' Capting Adair; so you need n't be mindin' that squall, though it 's more than a squall it 'll be."

" Why, will it be a storm? "

" It 'll blow hard annyway. A squall, an' then a squall on the back o' that, an' then a blow, an' a bigger blow! That 's what it 'll be. I know thim summer storms that come out o' the south."

" Do you advise anything? "

" Aye, aye, Capting Wester. I 'd advise ye to be aisy about the sail we carry. There 's a good deal more on her now than the *Hooroar* 'll stand, — an' the less the better, as Moriarty used to say av thim immoral bally-dances at the Royal Cork Theayter."

"Well, do as you think best. Hillo — that's strange; there's not only a swell, but a short choppy sea on, and yet there's no wind to speak of."

"True, for you, Capting Wester, mum. That's the way it comes whin it's going to *blow*."

"She'll have her nose in that choppy water before long," Honor interrupted, with a warning gesture. " Had n't we better shift the jib, and reef the bowsprit? That'll save the weight at her bows."

" Aye, aye, mum."

Almost without a moment's warning a squall leaped across the water, and sprung at the sails of the *Belle Aurore*.

The yacht reeled under the impact, and then righted, shivering all over.

"Now then, let go the outhaul," shouted Mrs. Moriarty. "That's right! Look alive, Lanigan, and let go these halyards — look out, look out there — keep the sail down on deck to leeward of the mainsail! O'Leary, you help Lanigan to reef the bowsprit. Polly, you cut along with O'Leary, and untoggle the sheets, unhook the tack and head from the outhaul and halyards, and fasten tight to the cleats! Miss Macfee, put the helm up, and let us run before the wind."

"Aye, aye, mum."

It was thus that Mrs. Moriarty proved she was really first-officer. Miss Macfee herself admitted, in the privacy of her thoughts, that one could have done no better; indeed, that, in an emergency like a squall she could not have skippered so well.

"Slack off the lee-runner! Look out, there! Here's a squall comin'! Miss Macfee, you come here, plase an' lind a hand. Capting Adair, mum, an' Capting Wester, plase God by takin' that wheel an' kapin' us as stiddy as a bathing-machine on the sands."

With the sudden onrush of the squall the water seemed to rise up all round the *Belle Aurore*, which was now surging heavily forward. The lee gunwale leant over further and further, and the spray flew hissing from just beneath it.

"Quick there, you haythen divils! Trice up the tack an' lower the peak!"

While this was being done, Mrs. Wester turned with a furtive smile to her companion.

"So, after all, we are learning what it is to scandalize the mainsail!"

"Are we, dear! then the sooner this scandal is disproved the better! Oh, there it comes, worse than ever! Ugh!"

The last exclamation was because of a sudden flaunt of a wave over the stern, with a shower of spray right over Honor's shoulders and down her shivering neck.

"We'll 'av' to sail under the foresail only, Captings, if this goes on, — that, an' just a suspicion o' the mainsail."

"As you like, Mrs. Moriarty."

"As you will, Mrs. Moriarty."

Who says there cannot be unanimity between two captains on board one vessel?

The *Belle Aurore* now began to feel the jump of the sea. Neither Honor nor Leonora had had much experience in steering, save in smaller boats, and they gave too many hostages to fortune.

The sea had risen with extraordinary rapidity. A loud and increasing splashing was heard everywhere, as the waves slapped each other noisily. The wind had a howl in its shrill music. All the sky now was white and grey, except westward, where heavy bulbous black clouds impended and seemed overcharged with rain, thunder, and pent wind-bursts. It was one of those sudden storms that sweep up the Irish Channel, — violent eddies, often, from some heavy Atlantic gale sweeping past the Old Head of Kinsale but keeping seaward as long as the Irish coast lay a-lee.

"Honor," cried Leonora, between two swirling gusts of wind, that made the yacht spring forward as though she were a high-bred lashed by a whip: "Honor, what was it that Jacob Macmasters said about the *Belle Aurore* kicking up her heels?"

"I don't remember, dear; but if she won't do more than kick up her heels I'll be glad. I'm afraid she is going in for an abandoned skirt-dance."

"That wretched man said something about her rolling powers? I'm bound to say that she seems to me to be giving way to that weakness more than there's any need for. *Oh!*"

A lurch had precipitated one captain against the other.

Honor noticed that, despite the fresh wind and the flying sea-spray, Leonora was rather white. Furtively she rubbed her own cheeks. "What's the matter, there?" she cried, anxiously, as, just then, Lanigan's tall bony figure lumped across just aft the mast, — with what seemed the corpse of one of the crew hanging limply to right and left of her.

"It's Polly Jones, plase yer honors. She's as sick as a biled owl ahlready, drat her!"

"Oh, poor child! See that she has something, Lanigan!"

"I will that, by all the Sints," Lanigan muttered: "I'll see she gets the best skelping she's had since she slipt with a pittycut, if she's sick while I'm carrying her!"

But alas, the time was at hand when no kindly offices were to be thought of, when the world would shrink to the blank indifference of individual misery.

"Honor, dearest," — ah, the tremulousness of the captainly voice which had made so brave a show that morning, with sea-lore wonderful! — "Honor, dearest?"

"Yes, Nora?"

"Dear, are you sure you should n't go below? You — you — don't look quite yourself; and of course this rolling and tossing *is* a little trying."

"Oh, thank you, Nora — I — I *like* it."

The ghost of a smile came into the wan face of Captain Wester. The opportunity that had come was too good to be lost.

"Well, I 'm glad of that. For I am rather — eh — rather *cold*, and think I 'll go below just to put on some warmer clothes."

But she was forestalled.

Miss Macfee had seen how matters stood, and had come to the rescue. Honor had succumbed; abruptly, without thought of captainly dignity, Leonora, the crew, the yacht's fate, her own life or death, Wilfrid's happiness, the end of the world, the last trump, and the saving of her immortal soul.

Pride, combined with the absolute need

to stand by the helm till Miss Macfee — who was acting Samaritan to the prostrate Honor — returned from the cabin, sustained Mrs. Wester.

With weary eyes she caught a glimpse of what looked a small black cloud rising out of the sea, far to the northward.

"What is that?" she cried, gaspingly, to Mrs. Moriarty, who passed near at that moment, proud of her sea-legs, her knowledge of what to do, and of the magnificent confidence in her of all on board.

"That, Capting? That's Ailsa Craig."

"Oh, then we'll soon be in?"

"In, mum? In where?"

"Oh, wherever we're going to, you silly woman."

"Silly woman, indade! Bedad, — ah, I see, por thing! It's onaisy you're beginning to feel. Ah, Miss Macfee, there you are! — just give a hand here to the Capting — I'll see to the steerin'!"

And with that, Captain Wester was half guided, half lifted to the cabin, where already the groans of Captain Adair suggested the terrors of martyrdom.

"Are you ill, dear? are you very ill?" gasped Leonora, solicitously.

"No — no — not at all; but I 've a head-ache, a splitting headache!"

"Oh, so have I," and with that Mrs. Wester flung herself on the cabin sofa, too wretched even to attempt to reach her bunk.

Unfortunately, Mrs. Moriarty proved a true prophet. The squall passed, but only to be followed immediately by one still more severe. Within an hour the thunder-clouds came up, and with them the gale.

The yacht was now in the trough of the seas and rolled heavily. Not even the skilled steering of Bridget O'Leary, who had man-aged sloop, coble, or wherry in many a rough sea off Queenstown and down by Kinsale, could save the *Belle Aurore* from some bad plunging.

By the late afternoon half the crew were ill.

Fortunately, Mrs. Moriarty, Miss Macfee, and O'Leary were able to brave it out. Doubtless the certainty that the yacht would founder if *they* gave in, helped to keep them in good heart. But with Lanigan, Murtagh,

and Polly Jones incapacitated, and Miss
Macfee herself grimly wretched, there was
no one to attend to the captains.

For a long time Honor and Leonora suf-
fered in silence, except for expressive moans.

Courage, however, came to Mrs. Adair
through sheer desperation. With a great
effort she rose, staggered across the cabin,
and was half way up the stairs when she saw
the oilskinn'd bulk of Mrs. Moriarty looming
across the wet and stormy sky.

" O, Mrs. Moriarty," she cried pitifully,
" are we near anywhere? "

" Yes, Capting, darlint, but don't worry
your poor silf."

" But where are we? "

" Well, to be sure, we 're jist off Ailsa
Craig; and a pretty stiff gale it is."

" Oh, land us there ! that will do nicely ! "

" Land ye on Ailsa Craig ! Faith, Capting Adair, mum, if ye were birds we could
hardly land ye ! It 's only a rock it is, with
foothold for a rabbit or two."

" But is there no port near? "

" Well, yis, indade there is; there 's Ayr
an' Troon, an' if we keep on as we 're goin'

now, we might sail up the High Street of Ardrossan."

" Oh, Ardrossan. Yes, yes, let us go there. That is the place where we meant to write from."

" Ye may mean it, mem," broke in Miss Macfee, turning a white grim face upon her fellow-sufferer; " but it 's no Ardrossan ye 'll be seein' this night, I 'll warrant."

" Why not, woman?"

" Weel, mem, ye maun just as weel speak ceevil tae a body who 's nigh as far gone wi' the sickness as yersel."

When angered, Miss Macfee dropped into a broader Scotch than usual, and her tones became hard. But now there was excuse for her. To be sea-sick, and to be asked an unreasonable question, and, above all, to be called a " woman," — that might well try the patience of a saint, even of a good Presbyterian one.

But Honor was also at her last gasp. She could stand no more. With a groan she lapsed from her hold of the stair-rail, swung round, collided with the sofa whereon Leonora lay yearning for home, her husband,

and her child, and fell, at last, inert and in
utter collapse, upon her bunk.

She brought with her, however, a breath
of the fresh salt air. Momentarily revived,
Leonora likewise took heart. Alas, though
she actually staggered as far as the wheel,
the result was the same, and even more ex-
peditiously. Still, she succeeded in learning
from Miss Macfee that with the gale blowing
from the quarter it was, the yacht would not
be able to make for Ardrossan. The desti-
nation now was Lamlash Bay, in the Isle of
Arran.

With the hope that that goal would be
reached in an hour or two both adventurers
plucked up a little heart. Naturally a little
recrimination embittered the interjaculations
which did duty for conversation.

"But Leonora," — began Honor, after a
short lapse wherein both had other matters
to think of.

"Oh, what is it now, Honor?"

" Leonora, if as you say you are not really
seasick, can't you *do* something?"

"Can't I *do* something? O Honor!"

"Yes, I repeat; can't you do something — do *something?* Can't you lash the helm?"

"Lash the helm, Honor Adair? Why I tell you it's been trying to lash *me!*"

A deep groan, of suffering, not of sympathy, was the sole response.

"Honor!"

"O what is it? Why don't you go away? Why don't —"

"I — I — am so — so — so *tired* — so *tired,* I say, that —"

"Once and for all, Leonora, understand that I will not get up, — not though you were the Last Trump!"

With a sob Mrs. Wester buried her face in the sofa-pillow.

"You might at least say I was — *hic-ugh!* — say I was —"

"I'll say *anything,* Nora darling, if only you'll get me some hot tea."

"Hot tea! — and a moment ago you called me the Last Trump!"

"No, no, Nora dear, — the Angel that *blew* the last trump!"

"Well, all I can say is that if that last trump comes to us at sea, I hope there won't be as much blow along with it as there is at present ! ''

" O Leonora, if you can joke — and make such a wretched, wretched pun — I — ''

" How could it help being wretched, when *I* am wretched ? ''

But here an interruption occurred, in the shape of a wild yell from the stentorian throat of Bridget O'Leary, who was still at the helm.

" *Man overboard!* "

" O how dreadful ! " Honor cried, as she staggered to her feet, her eyes filled with horror. " O Nora, who can it be ?   This is a horrible end to our trip.   Quick, get up, dear !   We must give all the help we can ! ''

" Yes — yes — but one moment, darling. There 's no *man* to *go* overboard.''

" Ah — I never thought of that — but Bridget must simply have used the phrase — Oh, be quick — and let us help each other to go on deck ! ''

As they mounted, the keen air revived them somewhat. The dreadful fear, too, at their hearts drove sickness out of their minds.

Who could live in that wild sea, thrashed with foam as it was, and covered with whirling waves like leaping wolves? Even if the poor woman — or was it the girl Polly? — could swim, there would be no hope, with the yacht going before the wind like a greyhound!

The first thing they saw was Bridget's face, with the tears streaming from her eyes.

"Oh, what is it — who is it, O'Leary?" cried Honor, gaspingly.

"*Drowned — drowned,*" wailed Bridget, while she struggled with the helm.

"Is it Miss Macfee? O yes, it's poor dear Miss Macfee — I don't see her anywhere! Mrs. Moriarty — Mrs. Moriarty! — is it Miss Macfee that is drowned, is it Miss Macfee that has fallen overboard?"

"Oh, dear, no, Capting Adair, mum. Miss Macfee is jist av the idge av a tumbler o' steamin' 'ot, without sugar an' a slice o' lemon."

Mrs. Wester javelined the unfeeling wretch with her gaze.

"Indade, Capting Wester, mum, ye naden't be looking at me like that. There's no great harm done at all at all, except to the poor baste that 's drowned, God save the soul av him !"

"*Him — him* — Oh, was there a man on board after all?   Is it Jacob Macmasters?"

"Hould hard, Capt'n Wester, or you 'll be blown into the say !   See here, Capting darlint, excusin' the liberty, — jist claw on to me, as though you were a young lobster at its first tay-party and feelin' shy av all the big crabs an' the loike."

"O Mrs. Moriarty, what is this awful mystery?   Don't joke about it.   Tell us what it is !   *Who* has been swept into a watery grave?"

"Well, indade, my dear, it 's just Mayphisty !"

"*Who*, Mrs. Moriarty?"

"Jist the cat, darlint.   Come now, Mrs. Adair, mum, ye 're not fit to be up here ye are, and ye sick as a pleeceman when he sees the mad bull comin' out av the chaney-shop."

"*Just the cat.*   O Honor !   Just the —"

And with that, Captain Wester went into hysterics.

Choking with laughter, out of sheer relief, and filled with anxiety for Leonora, Honor forgot all about her sickness. By the time her dear colleague was brought round, she was still weak and staggery, but was able to look about her without nausea, and even able to inhale the salt breath of the foam-white sea.

Besides, a glance, and a word from Mrs. Moriarty encouraged her.

Arran was within sight. The island lay, a huge black splatch, well to leeward; but, so Mrs. Moriarty said, they would be past Pladda in less than half an hour, and soon thereafter be in the calm strait between the Holy Isle and Lamlash.

"Oh, Honor, tell me all!" murmured Leonora, still half-unconscious of all that had happened.

"Darling, poor dear Mephisto is drowned. He was swept out of the cuddy while he was stealing the cream. It is very sad — but — eh — *the rest of us are safe!*"

CHAPTER XI

FOR a wonder Mrs. Moriarty was a true prophet, for in less than an hour the *Belle Aurore* raced past the rock of Pladda. Almost immediately thereafter, despite the heavy swell, the yacht eased off somewhat. A look almost of daring came into the white faces of the two captains. After all, what did a little sickness matter, — that is, when it was over.

They had come through their first storm well. Not a spar lost, not a sail rent, only some fur scattered, and the soul of Mephisto let loose into the universe. Unfortunately the approach to Arran was veiled by driving mist. Honor and Leonora standing arm in arm close to the taffrail could hear the surge of the waves beating against the rocks; but they could see nothing of the mountains which rose majestically out of the sea. Once as they swept across Brodick Bay, they

caught a momentary glimpse of Goatfell
towering above the village of Brodick: but
in a few seconds the scene was again one
blur of driving rain and mist and sea-foam.
That glimpse, however, had filled them with
an intense nostalgia for the land. O comfortable cottages with red, warm hearths and
kettles of boiling water, and teapots filled
with that luxury at present unattainable;
and above all, with floors that did not give
and move about with maddening uncertainty!
Who would not be a cottager in preference
to any other human fate? Some such
thought as this flashed through the mind of
both Honor and Leonora. The latter leaned
closer to her friend, whispering: "We shall
soon be ashore, shall we not, darling?"

Again for a brief while, there was a nasty
toss as the yacht took the heavy surge, for
unfortunately Miss Macfee had mistaken
the exact lie of the land, deceived no doubt,
by the mist. It was necessary to put back
and tack in order to gain the entrance to
Lamlash Sound. This was indeed a bad
time to go through. All on board nearly
followed the fate of Mephisto, for at the

most crucial moment the tired Bridget
slipped and sprawled headlong on the deck,
with the result that the wheel flew round,
and the yacht was within an ace of founder-
ing. But if Miss Macfee had fallen in the
esteem of everybody by her exasperating
miscalculation, she redeemed it by the expedition with which she saved the situation.
Another hour passed, alas, before the yacht
came under the lee of the Holy Isle : an
hour wherein the sufferings of the much
tried captains were vividly reproduced, and
wherein the last vestige of regret for the
vanished Mephisto ceased to trouble. But
at last the sweep of the wind was cut off by
the towering bulk of the Holy Isle. Almost
before Honor and Leonora realized it, they
were aware of the sudden cessation of the
leaping and rolling of the strained vessel.
What an exquisite relief it was as the *Belle
Aurore* glided swiftly in that white and
stormy dusk, through the calm strait which
divides the Holy Isle from the waist of Arran.

. . . .

The beauty of the morning seemed doubly
beautiful after the horrible experiences of

the day before. Never had either Honor
or Leonora seen a lovelier spot. The low
cottages of Lamlash, clustered close to a
shore fringed with wood and thicket, beyond
which rose swelling hills clothed with wonderful velvety light; and above these again
the flanks and peaks of the mountains of
Arran. In the beautiful bay itself, nearly a
score of vessels of all kinds rode at anchor:
windbound foreign ships for the most part,
though no fewer than five yachts, yawls, and
schooners and small ten-tonners, lay in close
proximity. A few hundred yards seaward,
the Holy Isle rose sheer and isolate. The
water on its landward side was foamless and
almost quiet, though all around its front the
sea was still dashing its masses of yeasty
waters against the fanglike reefs and ledges.
The swift high voice of the wind could be
heard calling across the open sea, and the
noise, a subdued thunder, of the billows racing past the great cave known as the cell
of St. Molissos.

However, even the sea outside was nothing like what it had been. The water was
all blue or sunlit green, and though frothed

everywhere with white sheep, was no longer
disturbed by more than what is called a
land-lubber's gale. Hardly that indeed, for
every few minutes the actual force of the
breeze slackened, and it was clear a calm
would prevail by noon.

All that day, however, the luxury of the
rest was too great to be interfered with.
The temptation to go ashore, to wander into
that beautiful island, which now as in the
days of Ossian is the isle of romance, was
great : but greater still was the temptation to
be less romantic and to stay on board and
sip coffee and smoke cigarettes.

Besides, the brief spell of fine weather did
not last. With the noon calm the rain came
down. As has been truthfully observed,
when it rains in Arran it rains in the most
unmistakable manner possible. Honor and
Leonora were soon driven below. But oh,
the difference in that dainty cabin now.
Yesterday hateful because of the sufferings
endured there, to-day once again fair and
sweet, and lacking only the flowers which
Lanigan and Murtagh would fetch when
they returned in the dingey, which had

been despatched to Lamlash on a foraging expedition.

To sit still or lounge, to smoke and chat, to be able to read or write, or do nothing at all ! What a luxury and delight ! There was not even a faint heave or lift to be felt anywhere. The yacht might have been in a canal.

> " Port after stormie seas,
>   Death after life, doth greatly please," —

says the old poet, and truly enough few pleasures are equal to those of a safe and delightful haven after marine discomforts on a yacht that is in the habit of kicking up her heels.

Perhaps it was an undue confidence that made these two brave captains forget their recent woes, and laughingly assure each other that the next breeze they encountered — they called it ' breeze ' — would find them inured, and merrily secure upon their sea-legs.

It was a pity for them that the rain prevented their going ashore ; at least, so they said. It was certainly no pity for Richard

P. Wester and Wilfrid Adair; these gentlemen were each favored with an epistle. In
these epistles facts were done to death with
the most daring audacity. Exquisite hyper-
boles flaunted bravely across each page. A
"J" pen and a "Lady" pen concurred to
play havoc with the truth. For, alas! no
word was written that told of anything that
might be turned against the writer. All had
gone well; no laughter, no jibe, no furtive
smile, had haunted the start; no qualm had
crossed the mind of either adventurer; no
such able crew had ever sailed the Irish
Channel; and never, certainly never, had
two ladies so well withstood so rough and
wild a sea, neither having had a single
moment of discomfort nor. even guessed that
such a dire complaint as sea-sickness occasionally waylaid the unwary traveller.

It was a pleasure to write these letters,
and to reflect upon the envious longing of
Richard and Wilfrid. Well, if the letters
took those arrant husbands away from the
seductions of London, so much the better!
They were there on false pretences, the
wretches; were they not forgetful of two

beautiful wives they had left to mourn in the company of the Rev. James and the parish doctor? Now indeed they would discover that wives in exile could be as alluring and unattainable as sweethearts under a parental ban.

Written and duly addressed, the precious, if appallingly untruthful, notes were despatched in the dingey to the tiny building which did duty as post-office in Lamlash. At the pier-head lay the steamer, her engines still snorting, and a trail of black smoke still crawling from her funnel, which had arrived a brief while before; to remain till an hour after sunrise on the morrow, when, with urgent mails — and, as Leonora remarked, superfluous males — she would leave for other Arran ports, and thence across the Firth to Ardrossan. It was delightful thereafter to reflect on that orgy of mendacity. A wise French philosopher has remarked that women are never so profoundly happy as when they are telling the man they love an untruth. How jubilant, then, Mrs. Wester and Mrs. Adair, when they could hug to themselves the solace that, to their beloved, they had told not one, but a whole vivid budget of amazing inveracities!

Next morning, it was arranged, sufficient sail was to be hoisted to enable the yacht to steal out of Lamlash Bay; so that somewhere, according as wind and tide permitted, the two sea-lovers might again have the delight of a sunrise bath and a long, wave-buoyant swim.

Never had they slept so well, — the profound, dreamless sleep which can only follow the doing something we ought not to have done. It was joyful news when Polly Jones — now rubicund once more, and supremely happy because of the treat in store for her when the ladies should jump unguardedly into that sea which had so many terrors for her — a delight it was when the beaming Polly informed the still drowsy captains that a glorious morning had dawned. The sea was calm, she said, with just enough breeze to slide a yacht out of the Sound. Already they felt the slow motion. While they sipped their waking-cups of tea, mere hints of the banquet to follow, the *Belle Aurore* slid out beyond the west rocks of the

Holy Isle and round the promontory of King's Cross.

What a delight it was to leap into that sun-warmed water, — azure as far as the eye could reach, though green under the keel of the yacht ! It added to their enjoyment that the breeze had now completely fallen ; at least, at the spot where the yacht lay becalmed. Just beyond the headland of King's Cross a strong catspaw played, but even that was intermittent and added a zest to the glistering sheet of sea around.

The swimmers were adventurous. Safe in their imaginative security, they raced each other joyously, playing at dolphins, — mermaids indeed, sea-sirens such as Ulysses and his crew could never have resisted.

But suddenly Honor swung her arms with a backward sweep, and stood treading the water, breast high.

"What is it, Honor, what is the matter?"

"*Nora !*"

"Well, Honor, do speak out. Surely, *here* you are not seasick."

"Nora, have you noticed that we are drifting rapidly?"

" What then? "

" That we are drifting rapidly, and that
the yacht is becalmed — and — oh, Nora,
the dingey is ashore with Lanigan and Mary
Murtagh ! "

" Well, but, Honor — "

" Oh, Nora, don't you understand? We
are drifting, I tell you, — there's a current carrying us seaward, and those on
the yacht can do nothing to help us !
The yacht's becalmed, and the dingey is
ashore, and we'll be drowned, I know we
shall."

" Wait a moment, Honor," Leonora cried,
her face suddenly white ; " it can't be so.
In this calm sea we can easily swim back
to the yacht. Come, don't let us be
frightened ; let us give way with a will,
and keep together, and we'll be there in
no time."

But, alas ! there are currents in the deep
sea that will respect no swimmers, however beautiful. And the strong current that
sweeps off the Holy Isle and trends seaward,
in a great curve, had caught the two swimmers ; it was clear, not only to themselves,

but to those on board, that fate had caught the daring captains in what seemed like to be a fatal grip.

Good swimmers as they were, they kept their self-possession for a time. As long as there was hope that they might swim against, or evade the under-drift of the current, they held bravely forward. In a minute or two, however, it became evident that all attempts to reach the yacht would be unavailing.

Then, with one of the deepest instincts of womanhood, they screamed !

In the circumstances, it was much the most common-sense thing to do. "When you see you are going to be drowned, scream ! " is an admirable maxim. Honor and Leonora saw it, and they screamed.

No good came of this painful exercise. Indeed, it seemed as though a dangerous expenditure of much-needed breath was the sole result. A grim look came into the fair faces. It was no time for tears, and both women were brave as the bravest, and made of grit through and through. If they had to die, they had to die. But they would make a hard fight for it. There was a look in Honor's gray-green eyes and about Leonora's taut lips which showed they were not going to sink as long as a breath sustained them. As they swam slowly together, the utmost they could do was not to drift noticeably further away. It was some comfort to be in such proximity that they could speak without raising the voice.

Even in that moment of dire peril, the grotesque irony of life did not spare them. Indeed, why "spare" since irony is the saving grace of death as of life?

"Honor," gasped her friend, "I wonder what Dick and Wilfrid will think of our letters when they know that we are lying at the bottom of the sea?"

"Wilfrid always declared he never would go into mourning," said Honor mournfully, with a latent sob in her throat.

After this there was silence for a while. Suddenly, Mrs. Wester raised her head and stared fixedly at the *Belle Aurore*.

"What in Heaven's name is Bridget O'Leary doing, Honor?"

"Oh, Nora, she is *keening!*"

"*Keening*," repeated Leonora, awestruck. "Oh, Honor, is it so bad as that?"

And, indeed, on the deck, beside the wheel, the corpulent O'Leary was upon her knees with her hair streaming over her shoulders, and her arms upflung.

"Oh, wirra asthore" she wailed. "Oh, wirra asthore, wirra asthore."

The loud melancholy keen floated across a calm water, a fitting requiem for those whose fate now seemed sealed.

"Honor," whispered Leonora with a gasp.

"Yes?"

"Can you hold out a bit yet?"

"Yes."

"Ought n't we to pray — or — or — do something?"

"*I* can't, Nora: Oh, Will, Will, Will!"

The cry had contagion in it.

"Oh, Dick, Dick!" wailed the drowning spouse of that distant Lothario.

"Don't cry, Nora dear: if we've made donkeys of ourselves, we 'll die game!"

"I 'm *not* crying: it 's the salt in my eyes. Oh, —" and here a burst of tears and choking sobs nearly drowned the far spent speaker.

Neither had noticed that Bridget O'Leary had suddenly sprung to her feet and was no longer keening with all the eloquence of an abandoned banshee. Instead, she was wildly waving a red flag. At last the flaunt of this signal caught Honor's gaze. She slipped her head and shoulders above water, and took a good look round.

Behind her, not three hundred yards away, a yacht was bearing full upon them, coming slowly forward upon a catspaw of wind that had scurried around the headland.

As for those on the *Sea Hawk*, for so the savior vessel was named, there was nothing but stupefaction. They had not caught sight yet of the swimmers: all they saw was a yacht whereon a female behaved with extraordinary and convulsive gestures. It is unusual for yachtsmen to perceive a stout female waving a red flannel petticoat at the stern of another yacht on a morning when the sea is as calm as a mirror.

Still greater was their amazement when the despairing Bridget, fearing that the yacht

thus mercifully coming to the rescue would
slip past the drowning ladies, ran up her
extensive blood-red garment to the masthead,
and there jerked it to and fro.

The two gentlemen who stood by the helm
of the *Sea Hawk* looked at one another with
bewildered eyes.

It was at this moment that the man coiling
a halyard on the foredeck, called out, —

"Two swimmers ahead ! — Port the helm."

This done, the two gentlemen advanced
to see if help were needed. The taller of the
two, a man with a military air, had a glass
with him. He adjusted this to his eyes, and
almost immediately dropped it.

"By God !"

"What is it, Lascelles?" asked his companion eagerly.

"Look, Ruthven."

The younger man addressed took the
glass and stared through it.

"Well, I'm — "

Then, handing back the glass, he whistled
softly.

"Lovely, are n't they?" remarked the
elder *sotto voce*.

"Yes," answered the younger dreamily.

"Hexcuse me, gentlemen," broke in the sailor, who had first drawn their attention to the swimmers, "them air ladies as is floundering about out there will be drowned in another minute or two. They're caught in the current, they are, an' I reckon they've been drifted away from their yacht."

"By Jove, the man's right," exclaimed the elder yachtsman. "Quick, Douglas, I see what it is ; they've no boat on that yacht there, and these ladies will be drowned to a dead certainty if we don't get them out of this in a jiffy."

With the utmost expedition, the boat which trailed behind the *Sea Hawk* was hauled alongside. The two gentlemen sprang into it. The next moment they were oaring the pinnace swiftly towards the swimmers.

Of course Honor and Leonora had witnessed all this. Indeed, but for the sudden resurge of hope thereby caused, they might by this time have succumbed.

Nevertheless, as the pinnace drew near, their inherent pluck made them fight against adversity to the bitter end.

"Hello, there, ladies!" cried the elder of the two saviors. "I'm afraid you're in trouble? I hope you will let us aid you."

Gasping with excitement and exhaustion, both protested faintly that they were in no need of assistance.

However no subterfuges were now of any avail. The sea was indeed at their white drawn lips, and it was evident they could not hold out much longer.

"No," Leonora gasped, as the younger man tried to grab her by the hair. "We will not come on board."

"Then what the devil will you do?" exclaimed the young man perplexed beyond endurance.

How was he to know that the two beautiful young women, clad in the latest fashion in bathing costumes, did not care to clamber into a small boat and there, dripping and dishevelled, undergo the scrutiny of two fashionable exiles from a familiar world.

"What *will* you do?" he repeated.

Mrs. Wester's voice was very faint and far away as she whispered back; "You may tow us back to our yacht, the *Belle Aurore* yonder."

"Are you alone? Are there no men with you? You don't mean to say you are the skipper of the *Belle Aurore?*"

"No," answered Honor with a wan smile; "we are the skippers, — this lady and I."

"Oh!" said the young man, flabbergasted, "I see."

"Just so," added his companion, with a bewildered look.

Slowly the small boat jerked along the calm surface of the water. The two gentlemen rowed as men in a dream; all they could see above the thwarts of their boats were four white hands, which clutched desperately at the jerking gunwale as the pinnace made its slow way towards the *Belle Aurore*, over whose side Mrs. Moriarty impended her huge bulk behind which Bridget O'Leary regarbed herself in her flaming petticoat.

CHAPTER XII

WHEN, at last, the yacht was reached an unlooked for predicament occurred.

How were they to get out of the water. That problem seriously perturbed all that was left of the thinking powers of Honor and Leonora.

If they had objected to enter the pinnace, there was not less objection to an undignified scramble, as though of half-drowned rats, at the port gangway.

The situation was saved by Mrs. Moriarty.

"Gintlemen," she whispered in a hoarse voice that was audible over the yacht, and to the two ladies concerned as well as to their rescuers; "Gintlemen, for the love o' God turn the bright eyes av ye to the gyurls who are lookin' at ye from the bows. Thim dear ladies, nigh drownded, the Sints be praised for that ' nigh ' ! are onaisy with you lookin' at thim as though ye had never seen murmaids afore ! "

As the "gyurls" in question were Miss Macfee and the cabin-lass, it will be admitted that the "gintlemen" behaved with exemplary obedience, when they stared fixedly at the grim first officer and the dumpling-faced Polly, and gave not a glance at Mrs. Wester and Mrs. Adair, while these unfortunates were helped on deck by Mrs. Moriarty and Bridget O'Leary.

It was no easy task for Honor and Leonora to accomplish.

The moment they let go their hold on the gunwale of the pinnace they thought they would sink like stones. With a desperate clutch each regained their one link to safety. Not even when the strong arm of Bridget was round her waist was Honor able to struggle up the gangway, till at last the seemingly impossible was achieved, and she found herself prone on the deck of the *Belle Aurore.*

A few seconds later, Leonora was by her side, in the same plight. It was not till this

Wives in Exile

juncture that the rescuers ventured any comment; but now tongues were loosed.

"How are the ladies?" asked the elder gentleman, a tall thin military man, with grizzled hair, aquiline nose, and clear-cut features, a quiet smile on his handsome face.

The person to whom he addressed himself was Miss Macfee, who had gone to the bowsprit, and, having vainly waved for the slowly advancing dingey to make more haste, for neither Murtagh nor Lanigan would look round, had slowly returned to the side of the yacht, to watch suspiciously the movements of these unwelcome sea-rovers.

"My! ain't they 'andsome gintelmen," Polly had whispered ecstatically.

"Handsome is as handsome does," was the muttered response; "I dinna like thae fine birds. Canna they ha' the sense to gang back tae their ain boat, now that the leddies are safe an' soond."

"How are the ladies?" repeated the questioner.

"Hoots, sir, they're a' richt noo."

"Ah, I have the pleasure of speaking to a Scottish lady, I see."

After all, fine birds could sing a pleasant song. Miss Macfee was mollified, though she relaxed nothing of her grimness.

"Well, I dinna quite ken what that's got to dae wi' *you*, but if it's enny pleesure to know it ye 're welcome to the fac'."

"It is always a pleasure to meet a Scottish lady."

"Ye 'll no be frae the West yersel, I'm thinkin' ? "

"No, madam. I am an Englishman unfortunately. But my friend here is a Scot, and a good Scot too."

Miss Macfee looked closely again at the younger yachtsman, a handsome, fair-haired blue-eyed man, probably about five and thirty, tall, well set up, an Apollo, in comeliness, vigor, and lithe strength.

"Weel, ye mak a guid couple. I'll admit that."

"It is very good of you. We are grateful. And now may I ask again, how the ladies are? "

"They've jist gaun doon to the cabin. Puir things, they were nearer the kingdom o' heaven than they've ever been before."

The elder gentleman gave a short low laugh.

"Well, madam, it is n't the best way of getting there; though I should n't think that two such charming ladies — so young, and, if I may say so, so beautiful — could at any time be so very far away from the realm in question."

Miss Macfee stared grimly.

"Polly," she said at last, "rin doon to the cabin an' see how the leddies are. An' — Polly ! — "

"Yes 'm ? "

"Jist ask Captain Adair, or Captain Wester, if we 'll hae the yacht towed back into Lamlash Bay, — for the dingey will be here in a few meenits, an' it 's a deid calm noo."

"Captain Wester " — "Captain Adair " — what did it all mean? and Polly's " *Yes 'm ?* "

Who was this grim yachtswoman, and did the *Belle Aurore* have two captains? And where were the crew?

In the approaching dingey two women rowed. *Something* was up; what was it?

Thus pondered the two gentlemen.

"May I ask if the 'Captain Wester' and 'Captain Adair' you mentioned are the two ladies we had the pleasure of towing here?"

"Aye, jist so."

"Are they the captain — I mean the captains — of this yacht?"

"Ye maun be ain brither tae Tammas the Douter."

"No, no, my dear madam, I do not doubt you; but, eh, it is a little unusual, you know, for *two* captains to command a vessel, and for these captains to be ladies."

"Well, sir, I'm no for sayin' it isn't."

"And you, — may I venture to ask if you are a captain also?"

It was pleasant to be taken for a colleague of Mrs. Wester and Mrs. Adair, but prudence as well as native truthfulness counselled veracity.

"Na, na, I'm na a leddy at all. I'm first officer, though, an' stewardess inty the bargain, an' would now be in the cabin, but for — eh, here comes Polly the cabin-gurl."

The two men looked at each other blankly.

Was it a summer expedition from Bedlam,
— a cruise of harmless patients. Two captains, — and both ladies; the first officer a
woman, and stewardess as well as mate; the
cabin-boy a girl!

"Are you *all* women on board this — this
yacht?" demanded the younger man desperately.

"We are, sir; thet's to say, there are twa
leddies an' the ship's company."

"Are you all m — I mean, are you on a
cruise?"

"We are."

"And have you just left Greenock or
Dunoon, or somewhere on the Clyde?"

"Na, we hail frae Ireland."

"But you didn't come across the Irish
Channel in that gale yesterday?"

"Weel, it's jist what we did dae."

"And with a crew of women and two
lady-captains!"

"Aye, is there onything sae varry sur-
preesin' in that?"

"Yes, my good woman, there is."

"Oh, it is 'my good woman' now, is't?
An' ye wi' yer 'madams' an' 'ma'ams.' Oh,

weel, I bear nae malice. It 's the way o' the warl."

" No offence, no offence! Certainly not. I beg your pardon."

" Weel, 't is grantit."

" And what does Polly say? "

" She says the leddies are better noo."

" Do they send any message? We wait only to see if we can be of any service."

" Oh, they 'll get on fine, thank ye."

" H 'm. But —"

" Plase 'm ! "

" Weel, Polly, what is 't? " — Here a whispered colloquy took place.

" Sirs, the leddies send ye wurrd."

" Ah ! — what is it, if you please? "

" Captain Mrs. Wester, an' Captain Mrs. Adair send their respecs to Mr. ——, weel, I dinna ken wha ; an' to Mr. ——, it 's the same ow 're again; an' say that they 're mickle obleeged for their timely aid."

" May we come back and pay *our* respects to Mrs. Wester and Mrs. Adair? "

" Weel, I presoom ye may, sin' the leddies ask ye to favor them wi' yer company to lunch. An' Captain Adair would like tae ken if she's right in believin' that one o' ye twa gentry is Mr. Douglas Stuart, the Master o' Riven?"

A look of astonishment rewarded this communication.

"Yes, truly," said the younger man at last, "I am the Master of Ruthven. But—eh I did not have the happiness to recognise Mrs. Adair. Of course, the circumstances made it rather difficult to do so. Is she the dark or the fair lady?"

"The dark wan."

"And she is Mrs. Adair, you say. No, I don't — oh, wait a moment! Adair — *Adair!* I wonder if it's the wife of Wilfrid Adair, of something or other, — I forget its name, — in Ireland? He married some time ago, I know. I don't remember having seen his wife, but she may be known to me by her maiden name. Eh — ah — Miss — eh —"

"Miss Macfee!"

"Eh, Miss Macfee, — thank you. Can you tell me who Mrs. Adair was?"

"Na, sir, I can dae naethin' o' the kind. Ye can ask her yersel. It's no quite the thing tae be speerin' sic questions at me.

Shall I say ye 'll be here tae an early lunch-eon at twelve?"

"With the greatest pleasure. Pray assure the ladies that we would not dream of intruding, but it will give us very great pleasure indeed to accept their most kind invitation."

"Weel, I 'll gae the gist o't ennyway. I hanna' the geeft o' the gab sae promiscuous like."

"Then, at twelve, we shall be here again. Or is it the intention of Mrs. Adair and Mrs. Wester to return to Lamlash Bay? You may tell them that this calm will last all day, and perhaps till to-morrow; but that they will drift a mile or so seaward as long as the tide 's on the ebb, and after that more westerly."

"They 're jist gaun to bide where they are."

"Good-day, Miss Macfee! And good luck to the *Belle Aurore* and its gallant crew!"

So, the elder. The younger handed up two cards, and two from his companion.

With that the pinnace shoved off, just in time to avoid collision with the dingey, laden with vegetables and other comestibles, and oared by the perspiring Mary Murtagh and the bony Lanigan.

CHAPTER XIII

PUNCTUALLY as eight bells announced that noon had come, a boat put off from the *Sea Hawk*. In it were the two gentlemen, though now they were in the stern sheets, and the rowers were sailors.

They were well observed from the *Belle Aurore*. The two yachts lay becalmed, some four hundred yards distant from each other. The rumor of the femininity of the crew of the yawl had already spread throughout the *Sea Hawk*, a yacht of about the same tonnage. Amused eagerness showed itself on every face. Discipline, however, was strict, and none of the crew ventured to hope that visiting would become general!

When the boat was alongside, the visitors were met by Mrs. Moriarty. She beamed down upon them.

"Welcome to the *Bell Hooroar*, gintlemen," she began cordially, "an' — an' it's all roight the ladies are now, glory to God!"

"Good-day, ma'am! Are you the — the — "

" Indade, sorr, I 'm jist the first officer."

"The first officer? But the — the other — lady — informed us that *she* was first officer."

" An' that wis no lie either," replied Mrs. Moriarty, calmly.

" Are there *two* first officers, then, as well as two captains? "

"There is. Jist step this way, av ye plaise. An' may I be so bould as to ask which is the Curnel an' which is the other gintleman? "

"*I* am the other. This is Colonel Lascelles."

" Colonel Lascelles, Captings ! "

"The Master o' Ruthven, Captings ! "

The two gentlemen advanced, each hat in hand.

At close quarters they were even pleasanter to look upon than the ladies had found them on a first acquaintance. As for Colonel

Lascelles and his companion, if they said little, their eyes were eloquent.

Never had two such bewitching captains sailed the sea ! If they had seemed comely and even beautiful when half drowned, they now looked as though their perilous experience had given them back years of youth and beauty. Moreover, each had made the utmost of their store of apparel, and were now as trim and generally seductive as when, at the Royal Erin, in Dublin, a young commercial had given them his unstinted homage and admiration.

The two ladies rose from the deck-chairs whereon they were reclining, and received the visitors cordially.

"Now, how do you know that I am Mrs. Wester and not Mrs. Adair?" demanded Leonora with a smile.

"My dear Madam, your invaluable first officer — co-First-Officer Macfee — informed us that Mrs. Wester was the lady who was fair. But I do hope you are both now quite recovered? So far as looks go, if you will allow me to be so personal, I think we need have no anxiety ! It is not every one who could be nearly drowned in the morning, and be able to entertain guests at noon!"

"We are quite well, thank you. It *was* a little dangerous, swimming so far away from the yacht in a strange place. And now permit us to introduce ourselves, since our husbands are not here to do it for us. This is Mrs. Honor Adair, the wife of Mr. Wilfrid Adair, of North Mountmichael, in County Shannon. I am Leonora Danby, the daughter of the late Lord Curraghmore, of Mountmichael, and wife of Mr. Richard P. Wester, of Chicago and Brooklyn. And this is our yacht, — Mrs. Adair's and mine; and we are off on a cruise by ourselves, — and that is all!"

"It is an honor and a delight to meet you, my dear ladies. Let me also act as our own introducers, and tell you that my friend here is Douglas Stuart, the Master of Ruthven, and so eldest son of the Earl of Inveresk. I am Colonel Edward Lascelles, late of the Bengal Lancers, and now on furlough for a year."

"And now, Mrs. Adair," broke in the Master of Ruthven, with a pleasant South-

Scottish accent, "will you tell me how it is I am so fortunate as to have been recognized by you?"

"You have met my husband, I think?"

"Certainly. I have met Wilfrid Adair several times, some three or four years ago. The last time I saw him was at a Vice-Regal Ball at Dublin."

"I remember. And I have aged so much that you do not recognize *me*?"

The young man looked intently for a moment or two.

"Why, is it possible! You are Honor O'Connell, the daughter of dear old Terrence O'Connell, Squire of Tansor. Of *course*, I remember you now. And what a delightful evening we had at that ball! Oh, this is indeed a pleasure to meet Miss Honor O'Connell as Mrs. Adair of the *Belle Aurore*!"

With that the last fragment of ice gave way. Already an air of old acquaintance-ship prevailed.

For a time, of course, the conversation turned upon the voyage of the *Belle Aurore*, and on the adventurousness of the two captains. The visitors were delighted. They had never heard of anything so charming, Colonel Lascelles reiterated.

"Are you married, Colonel?"

"I am, my dear Mrs. Wester. I am. My wife is at present at Brighton."

"How would you like it if *she* went off like this?"

"Oh — eh — ah — well, you see my dear madam, Mrs. Lascelles is not very fond of the sea."

"But if she were?"

"Oh, of course I should be charmed — *charmed!*"

"I *wonder.*"

Hereat both Mrs. Adair and the Master of Ruthven laughed.

"Why do you laugh, Mr. Stuart?"

"Forgive me : but —"

"Oh, just so — I understand! Colonel, you are deceiving us! But now, here is Polly, to announce that luncheon is ready. Gentlemen, you must not expect much. We are anchorites, Mrs. Adair and I. We can promise you some good coffee, and if you are not shocked at ladies smoking we shall share with you some cigarettes which we think you will admit are as good as any you can get in London. I have them sent to me from America, — and I never smoke one but I think I am inhaling the very soul of our beautiful Virginia."

The luncheon proved to be a surprise number two, — or number a hundred!

It was most daintily set, and Mrs. Moriarty had brought her finest resources into play. The result was a repast which would have done credit to a Russian Grand Ducal yacht in the Mediterranean, or to the most "luxuriantly appointed" of the craft that congregate at Cowes during the season.

Long before the adjournment to the deck, both gentlemen had lost their hearts. Never were there such charming companions, so winsome, so gay, so amusing, so beautiful.

As for the circumstances, were they not unique?

The first sword of flame in this Eden upon the waters was when the third cigarette had been smoked by Mrs. Wester.

"And now, Colonel Lascelles and Mr. Stuart," she remarked nonchalantly, "we won't keep you. I am sure you are longing to return to the *Sea Hawk.*"

" Indeed we are not, Mrs. Wester! How can you even hint at such a thing ! "

" Well, we must perforce turn you out, then ! We don't want to be inhospitable. But really, you know, we have rewarded you quite enough for having saved our lives."

" We do not rate such precious lives at so low a valuation, — charming as that has been ! "

" Compliments won't save you, Colonel ! No, no, you must go ! Besides, Mrs. Adair and I have rather important letters to write, and we must get on with them at once."

" The decrees of the Medes and Persians ! Well, so be it. We submit. But is there any chance of your honoring the ocean in a similar way to-morrow ? "

" None. We have had our last swim in the open sea, away from the yacht."

" One favor ! "

" Granted — if a very, very small one. For myself I speak."

" Will you and Mrs. Adair honor us by a

return visit to afternoon tea, — better still, to
dinner?"

"Thank you, — but, no!"

"Oh, pray be generous! Mrs. Adair, I am
sure you will not be so cruel as Mrs. Wester.
Remember, my dear Mrs. Adair, that when
your mouth filled with sea-water, when you
first caught hold of our boat, I looked
away!"

Honor laughed.

"After *that,* you cut away one refusal. I
propose a compromise, Leonora. I agree
with you that we cannot go to dinner, as
Colonel Lascelles so kindly proposes, but we
ought, I think, to return his and Mr. Stuart's
call. So, shall we go to tea?"

"Yes, if the going and the coming and
the tea can all be included within one hour."

"Gladly," exclaimed both gentlemen, in
their eagerness.

"You are eager to limit us."

"No, no, Mrs. Wester — it is only that — "

"Oh, I understand, my dear Colonel
Lascelles. Now, there is your boat! We
cannot permit a longer visit. Our crew will
mutiny."

" One word, only! If ever you disband your crew, will you give me the option of engaging one member?"

" Miss Macfee?"

" No, my dear Mrs. Adair. Mrs. Moriarty."

" Mrs. Moriarty?"

" Yes. She would be a serious addition to the ballast of any small yacht, but she is simply invaluable as a cook. Madam, I would sail to perdition in such company, with such a cook!"

" You share the views of Mr. Wester and Mr. Adair!"

" H'm. It does n't look like it, — so far as *they* are concerned."

" No. The absent never know all that they miss. But they are good young men, and we shall be glad to greet them — to-morrow!"

Honor shot a glance at Leonora. It told all. Dissimulation was advisable, was it?

" To-morrow, Mrs. Wester? Oh, I hoped — we hoped — that — that — "

" We were wives in exile without the option of return?"

" No, certainly not, — but without the likelihood of reunion!"

"Well, now you know the truth."

"And are your husbands to meet you here?"

"Yes, here, or no — where is it, Honor?"

"At Ardrossan."

"Oh, Ardrossan. Perhaps we shall have the pleasure of meeting you there, for we also have made that a rendezvous for a possible addition to our small company."

"Did I say Ardrossan?" Leonora went on, calmly, with shameless audacity.

"Mrs. Adair did."

"Did she? How stupid! Honor, dear, don't you remember that we were to meet at Tarbert in Loch Fyne?"

"Yes, of course. I mistook the name. I was not sure whether it was Ardrossan in Loch Fyne or Tarbert in Ayrshire!"

It was the last mendacity.

The gentlemen shook hands, said *au revoir,* and reluctantly disappeared alongside the *Belle Aurore.* Before they shoved off, Colonel Lascelles looked earnestly at Mrs. Moriarty.

"Mrs. Moriarty! You may be a first officer and pilot, and I know not what all, — but you are also a *treasure.*"

" Indade, sorr, it 's verry kind o' you to say so. Poor ould Moriarty allus said the same."

" Did he? I do not wonder at it. Madam, my name is Edward Lascelles, Colonel Lascelles. If ever you want a berth as cook on board a yacht, — or as housekeeper, cook to a dyspeptic but ever sanguine Colonel, you have the address on this card to which to apply to."

" Thank ye kindly, sorr ; but I 'm born for the say, I am."

" You are born to make the best soufflé and the most delicious lobster salad it has ever been my lot to partake of. Good day — *madam !* "

" An' a hundred av thim to you — *sorr !* "

CHAPTER XIV

THE calm prevailed all day, though the sky became slightly overcast. A light breeze was probable at sundown.

At four o'clock the dingey of the *Belle Aurore* put off on the return visit.

Mrs. Wester and Mrs. Adair had exchanged their nautical raiment for a compromise, — costumes at once " sea-going " and after a more conventional kind.

A slight trepidation seized them as they listed alongside the *Sea-Hawk*. For one thing, the men on the foredeck grinned rudely as the dingey drew near. Their eyes were admiringly set not only upon the two ladies, rather humped together in the small dingey, but on Mary Murtagh and Bridget O'Leary.

Colonel Lascelles and the Master of Ruthven met their guests at the rope gangway.

Certainly the welcome was a cordial one. It was a pleasure to both ladies to be received with so much deference subtly compounded with admiration.

As for the dingey, — it was secured alongside and allowed to drift. Miss Murtagh and Miss O'Leary yielded to the pressing solicitations of the crew of the *Sea Hawk,* to join in " tay an' 'ot muffins."

Nevertheless, the meal — if meal it could be called which consisted only of tea, for none felt inclined to eat after the *Belle Aurore* luncheon — was rather a flat one. A certain constraint crept in, no one knew how, or just where it lay. But it was there.

Honor and Leonora both declined to smoke. Mr. Douglas Stuart took this mournfully, but his companion was more philosophical.

" Women," he muttered to himself, " women are the most incalculable of all God's creatures. We must endure. They are our cross — a delicious cross, but still a cross. Heigh-ho, when I was young — "

Etc., etc.

In a little while Mrs. Wester grew restless. Somehow or other she fancied that Colonel Lascelles looked at her with rather too conspicuous admiration; and as for the Master of Ruthven she wondered that Honor could sit unmoved under so adoring a scrutiny.

Providentially, a drop or two of rain fell from a passing cloudlet.

"I think we must be going, Honor. It is coming on to rain."

"Yes, we must." The words were spoken quietly and apparently quite indifferently, but Leonora rejoiced to know that her friend understood, and was as eager to make a move as she was.

"Now, Mrs. Wester, *do* stay. It will disappoint us tremendously if you go. We have got the divinest little dinner for you, — and we beg of you to stay and share it with us, and then gladden our hearts with some music."

"Thank you, Colonel Lascelles, but we must go."

"Oh, this is too bad for you, really! But at least let us act as your consort — the *Sea Hawk* is at your service in any way."

"Thank you again and again, Colonel: but the truth of the matter is that we want to run all our little risks by ourselves. There would be no triumph in meeting danger if we had such skilful sailors as Mr. Stuart and yourself at hand to look after us."

"Then at least let us meet again. May we — may we make a call upon you this evening, after dinner, just for a little music and a chat? Stuart, here, has a capital voice, and from what you tell me, Mrs. Adair must sing like an angel."

"No, *really*. We are both tired out. You *must* excuse us. The moment dinner is over, I want to lie down and sleep off all our fatigue and excitement, and I am sure Mrs. Adair is in the same condition."

"Yes indeed. And now we *must* go. Mr. Stuart, will you kindly ask our men — our women, I mean — to get into the dingey."

An uproarious shout came from forward at that moment. The Colonel frowned.

"Mary and Bridget are enjoying themselves, no doubt, but we must interfere with their fun. *Please*, Mr. Stuart."

" One word, dear Mrs. Wester. Are you going to remain in Lamlash Bay all night?"

"Certainly."

" Then may we have a farewell breakfast together, under the shadow of the Holy Isle?"

" Unfortunately, Colonel, we are going to sail at sunrise."

" But it may be wet. I am *sure* it is going to rain. And if so, of course you won't sail?"

"The weather makes no difference to us. Mrs. Adair and I are seasoned sailors."

" But surely you want to see something of Arran? It is a most beautiful island. I was going to propose that we make a climbing expedition up Goat Fell — or that we take a trap and go for a drive round the eastern coast to Glen Sannox, and over the mountain-road to Loch Ranza, — a superb drive, I assure you; probably the finest you have ever seen!"

"Thank you, dear Colonel Lascelles, but our *husbands* wish to see Arran with us. We are going to return with them, when we meet them at Greenock."

"At Greenock?"

"Yes — why not?"

"O, merely because I thought Mrs. Adair had said *Androssan,* and you *Tarbert.*"

A slight flush came into Leonora's face. But she restrained the laugh that was imminent.

"Did she? Did I? My memory is awful. So, as you will now see, Colonel Lascelles, we must be inhospitable. Ah, there are Murtagh and O'Leary. And now — good-by, and ever so many thanks for rescuing us in our predicament — and I *do* hope we may meet again, and soon. I know it will delight Mr. Wester to meet you, and thank you in person."

"Ah, very good of Mr. Wester, I'm sure; very good. But eh — my dear Mrs. Wester — What! you *must* go! Oh, well, alas, the best of friends must part!"

And so, at last, Captain Adair and Captain Wester bade farewell to their companions.

At the final moment weakness overcame Honor. Laughingly she promised that if in the morning the *Belle Aurore* were still in Lamlash Bay, or at Tighnabruaich in the

Kyles of Bute, which latter she and her friend had expressed a wish to see, — that, in either event, the gentlemen would be welcome at breakfast.

As the dingey was rowed away, — to a spontaneous cheer from the crew of the *Sea Hawk*, whose hearts had been won not only by the blonde Mary and the rubicund Bridget, Mrs. Wester whispered in her colleague's ear, —

"Dear, you should n't have done that. It 's all very well, so long as it does not go too far; but neither Colonel Lascelles nor your friend Mr. Stuart are *angels*. And they both seem to think — they — both — seem — to — think —"

"What?"

"Well, dear, that we are n't exactly angels either!"

"Nora, my dear, you need n't in the least distress yourself."

"Why not?"

"*Because I have studied the geography of this island.*"

"Ah, — I *see!*"

CHAPTER XV

IT was a lovely evening; one of those soft velvety gloamings which are nowhere so beautiful as in the west coast of Scotland.

The bay — to which the *Belle Aurore* had returned — was absolutely calm. The only ripple upon the water was when small rowing-boats moved to and fro, their occupants fishing for liath and saith, or singing, or simply rowing about for the sake of the cool breath of night and the beauty of those still waters.

Darkly conical, the Holy Isle rose up like a black cloud, till the moon came out and revealed it in its barren beauty, softened to a new and strange loveliness.

At the pier at Lamlash the red and yellow lights of a steamer flared unwaveringly, and every now and again the snort of steam came through the stillness. A relative stillness, for the bay was full of small boats and anchored yachts and coasters. Then, too, from the white row of cottages came many sounds: laughter, and faint cries, and the confused hum that, at such an hour in such a place, is always to be heard.

Inland, the bleating of sheep was audible. From a clachan somewhere behind Lamlash, the thin wailing notes of the bagpipes thrilled upon the air.

Seaward, westwardly, just where the moon, that had now sailed from behind Goat Fell, silvered a wide patch of water, a shoal of herring splashed.

It was an intense enjoyment to Honor and Leonora to sit quietly on the deck of the *Belle Aurore* and enjoy it all. There was, of course, a temptation to go ashore; still more, to get into the dingey and row about; but after all, the paramount temptation was to sit still, in exquisite absorption of all the beauty and mystery and charm.

Within a couple of hundred yards from them a large vessel, one of a line of Australian ships plying between the Clyde and Australia, lay waiting for the expected breeze that midnight or dawn would bring. Her decks were crowded by passengers, eager to enjoy this last beautiful glimpse of the land they were leaving.

"Sing to them, Honor," Leonora whispered suddenly, as she lifted the guitar that lay by the side of the deck-chair whereon she rested.

"Yes," answered Honor, simply, "but what, 1 wonder?"

"Oh, that song of your own that you call 'Farewell.' See, I will play the old air of 'The Wind in the Reeds;' that will just suit it."

The strong vibrant notes of the guitar swept across the water at a moment when there happened to be silence on board the ship. The effect was wonderful. In a few seconds rows of black heads and dark bodies were seen clustered along the starboard side of the emigrant vessel. Then Honor began her song, her beautiful voice, with its note of poignant tenderness, coming upon the night with a sweetness that brought a hush upon every one, and tears to many eyes.

"Where is the land
    We fain would reach?
On what far sea,
    To what far beach?

Wives in Exile

O longing heart,
  When shall there be
On what far strand
  Sweet rest for thee,
Sweet peace for me.
    For me
    And thee !

" 'T is far away
  That unknown clime !
A shadow lain
  In the shadow of Time,
But if at last
  That land we gain,
Ah, who shall say
  We 've crossed the main
And lost our pain,
Our old-world pain !
    Ah, farewell, pain,
    Ah, farewell, pain ! "

When she ceased there was absolute silence for a few seconds. Then, quite audibly, came cries for the singer to continue.

" Dear, that was a lovely song," whispered Leonora, "and you were right to sing it. Most of the poor people on board that emigrant ship will be just in the mood for so sad a strain. But now do sing something blither. Let it be that song that Wilfrid insisted on your singing at the picnic at the Giant's Causeway that glorious day of the gale."

With a loud clear ringing voice, filled with a certain proud abandonment, Honor sang to Leonora's vigorous accompaniment on the guitar : —

> " The south wind on the hill,
>   And the west wind on the lea, —
> But better than these I love
>   The north wind on the sea !
>
> " For the north wind on the sea
>   Is fearless and elate :
> The ocean vast and free
>   Is not more great.
>
> " On the hill the south wind laughs
>   Where the blue cloud-shadows flee :
> The west wind takes the mead
>   With a ripple of glee.
>
> " But the north wind on the deep
>   Is the wind of winds for me, —
> Spirit of dauntless life
>   And lord of liberty ! "

To the delight of both, the last verse came back with a refrain, followed by a glad cheer —

> *" But the north wind on the deep*
> *Is the wind of winds for me, —*
> *Spirit of dauntless life*
> *And lord of liberty ! "*

'They will remember that, Honor," Leonora cried exultantly, as the cheer swept across the bay ; " and though it is only a verse about the north wind, it will mean a breath of free life and liberty to live it, to some eager souls there. I am glad you sang *that!*"

But soon thereafter the bay became almost silent. One by one the lights of Lamlash were extinguished ; and before long only one or two lingered. On the calm water there were red eyes staring out into the darkness, the fore and aft lanterns of the many craft scattered the whole length of the Kyle of Lamlash between the headlands of Brodick Bay and Whiting Bay.

By midnight the expected breeze had not come, but in the moonlit sky a few frayed white drifts of vapor showed that wind was stirring on the high levels of the air.

Honor and Leonora were now below, having first given strict injunctions to

235

Miss Macfee that they should be called at dawn.

Miss Macfee, however, who knew the project entertained by the captains, took it upon herself to arouse them while it was still dark. " There's a nice breeze beginnin' tae blaw, mem," she remarked to Honor, who had sleepily responded to her summons, " an' we can slip oot o' the Bay as quiet's a mooss ! "

In a brief while the two captains were on deck. Thereafter a few minutes sufficed for the setting-sail and weighing anchor. The big emigrant ship had already done likewise, and was slowly forging ahead out of the bay.

It was easy to slip out under the lee of the *Loch Etive*, as the ship was named ; and as a matter of fact none on board the *Sea Hawk* noticed the *Belle Aurore*, as, obscured by the big sea-going ship, she slowly glided out into the open. Once there, it is true, she could be discerned clearly enough, sailing as she did on a southwestwardly course, as though for Ireland.

The moment, however, that the western headlands of the Holy Isle shut her off from view, the *Belle Aurore* swung round, and went off on a northeasterly tack. In twenty minutes she had swept past the Holy Island, and was making the foam dance on the beautiful stretch just outside Brodick Bay.

The soft rosy light of a lovely dawn made the mountainous centre of Arran inexpressibly lovely. The moon still hung in the west, a pale silver disk; and here and there a faint star lingered; but already the new day was come, and come in beauty.

Honor and Leonora walked to and fro, or sat for a time, entranced. Arran seemed an isle of dream; Goat Fell, rising vast and precipitous, had all the morning glory on his shoulders; behind, the serrated Peaks of the Castles were already torches of smouldering light.

In a moment these torches broke into golden flame. It was as though the sun had leaped up from Glen Sannox and scaled height after height till he reached those wild summits; and now, with a sudden mighty lift, he was over the ridge and had swung into the blue vault of heaven above the glowing hills.

"Honor, we *must* go ashore, if only to say that we have been in Heaven!"

"Gladly. Miss Macfee, what is that little promontory yonder, with the cluster of cottages?"

"That's Corrie, mem. A gae bonnie wee place. An' that's the inn ye see wi' the sun on it; a fine hoose, whaur the Duke himsel' micht be glad to stay, an' be as weel lookit after as at the Castle yonner."

"What duke?"

"What duke, mem! Dinna say sic a thing in Arran, or folk wud think ye dementit. There's only one duke possible to Arran bodies, — and that's Hamilton."

"Well, since his Grace does n't seem to appreciate Corrie we'll set him a good example. Let's lie to there, and get the dingey ready, and we'll breakfast at the inn."

"What about the *Sea Hawk*, Honor?" Leonora interrupted.

"We can race her if we see her coming! But as a matter of fact, I have just learned from Mary Murtagh — who had it from one of the crew — that Colonel Lascelles and his friend must be at Greenock by to-day or to-morrow, as they have chartered the *Sea Hawk* for a month only, and their time is up."

" Ah, — we shall see ! "

At this juncture the dingey came alongside, and soon the little boat was swaying in the tide against the smooth ledges of the rocky promontory.

How delicious was the smell of the land, with a poignant touch given to it by the peat-smoke that had begun to rise from some of the fishermen's cottages ; and with odors of moor and bracken and bog-myrtle blending with the keen breath of the seaweed. The air, too, was light and cool and exhilarating.

"What a heavenly spot!" Honor exclaimed, as they mounted the rocks, and looked at Corrie, with two or three brown fishing cobles in its little haven, and then, to their left, at the inn, — westward the wide stretch of beautiful coast to Brodick headland, at the end of which Holy Isle seemed to rise out of the sea. "Oh, what a heavenly spot! I *must* stay, and look at this wonderful view. Just look at the mainland yonder, — or, no, that is the island of Bute, I suppose; but see what wonderful lights and shadows! Nora, dear, you be an angel and go and order breakfast. I promise to come the moment you whistle!"

Mrs. Wester admitted that she was an angel to accede, and then acceded. Honor was still standing rapt in delight at the beauty around her, when her friend returned and touched her abruptly.

"What is it, Nora? Why, dear, you look as mysterious as though you were weighed down by some hidden crime or appalling secret! Are there no eggs, no bacon, no scones or butter or milk, no tea or coffee?"

"Quick, Honor, get into the dingey. There is not a moment to lose."

"Not a moment to lose! Why, what in Heaven's name do you mean, Leonora?"

But Mrs. Wester vouchsafed no reply. Silently the two ladies descended towards the dingey again. Every second or third step Mrs. Adair looked at her friend as though apprehensive concerning her reason.

Bridget O'Leary, who had rowed them ashore, seemed almost as astonished as one of her captains. However, she said nothing as both seated themselves.

"Shove off, Bridget! Row as hard as you can."

O'Leary gave a look of commiseration at the speaker, and then glanced knowingly at Captain Adair. The glance plainly said, "Poor thing, she's touched."

While they were yet half way to the yacht, Honor tried once again to elicit some information.

"What is it, Nora darling? Do tell me!"

"It's Nemesis."

"*Who?*"

"Nemesis. Two of them."

"Oh, Nora darling, has that horrible swim affected your head? Who is Nemesis, and, whoever he or she is, how can there be two Nemeses or Nemeseses or Nemesi or Nemesae, or whatever their horrid name may be in the plural?"

But again silence.

The yawl was recalled without delay. The moment she was on board Captain Wester ordered the anchor up.

Mrs. Moriarty looked at her blankly.

"Capting darlint, — " she began coaxingly.

"Don't be a fool, Moriarty."

"Indade, mum, if you'll be so good as to misremember — "

"Oh, all right, Moriarty: we have no time for talking about nothing. Have all sail set. We want to get round the Cock of Arran at once."

"Aye, aye, mum. Where for, then?"

"Up the Sound of Bute, and then across the Sound of Kilbrennan into Loch Fyne. We want to anchor in Loch Tarbert."

While sail was being set, Honor turned to her friend.

"Now, Leonora Wester, I insist upon knowing what all this means. As long as we were ashore I couldn't force you to speak if you didn't want to: but here we are *both* captains."

"Well, what then?"

"I could put you in irons, or at least arrest you, and of course the crew would support *me*, as they are all dying to know the secret."

"O'Leary has already made the most of her experience."

"You are a darling."

" In the ' little goose ' sense, Nora ? "

" Yes, but now that we are safe — "

" Oh, Nora, *safe!* Why, what do you mean ! — Ah, wait a minute, I see daylight ! "

" What 's your chink, Honor ? "

" Why, I suppose Colonel Lascelles and Mr. Stuart have either come over here last night, or else have seen our departure this morning and have crossed the waist of the island so as to catch us here ! "

" Ingenious enough till it's looked into, and then obviously absurd."

" Oh, don't speak with such an air of maddening superiority. If I am wrong in a very natural supposition, say so at once. I believe it is all a piece of bluff on your part, Nora ! "

" No, Honor. I will tell you why I stopped short. Just as I was talking to a handsome old lady who seemed to be lord (or lady) of all she surveyed, I glanced into the breakfast-room, and there, reflected in a mirror, I saw — "

" What ? — Your own startled face, you dear goose ? "

" No — I saw — "

" Well? — Well? — "

"*I saw Richard P. Wester and Wilfrid Adair!*"

" Good Heavens, Leonora," Mrs. Adair exclaimed, growing pale, " it *can't* be true! You were imagining ! "

"*I saw Richard P. Wester and Wilfrid Adair.* Richard was eating the marmalade from his plate with his tea-spoon : a habit I am familiar with. Wilfrid was helping himself to an amount of eggs and bacon that cannot be good for any human being."

Honor was convinced. There are traits that are more assuring than the testimony of angels.

" What can it mean, dear?" she asked in an awed whisper.

" Pursuit."

" Ye — es — yes — I suppose so."

" Unquestionably. I realized it in a moment. Yes, Honor, in a flash I saw what it was. Our telegrams gave them the necessary fillip. Probably, too, they found London not *quite* what they wanted ! — or that *they* were n't wanted ! They said they would chase us. Probably they came straight to Greenock. It's a wonder they did n't engage a yacht there. But I suppose they came on here first. Do you remember how we both raved about Arran ever since that dear girl, Edith Wingate, disclosed to us its beauties; and how we tried to make our spouses take us here; and how we swore an oath that it would be the first place in Scotland we should go to, if ever we got across the Irish Channel at all?"

"Yes, yes, indeed I do."

"H'm, by the way, — had n't Wilfrid a great admiration for Miss Wingate?"

"She admired him, I know."

"Ah, that is the same thing t' other way round. And Honor, do you know — what I for one had quite forgotten — that Edith Wingate comes here every summer, and lives somewhere near this very place?"

"Ah."

"Yes. Just so."

"And Richard P.?"

"Certainly *he* would not come to Arran because of the *beaux yeux* of Miss Edith Wingate! He admires blondes. A restricted taste, no doubt: but he was born that way."

Honor smiled.

"Dear," remonstrated her friend, "don't smile like that. It does n't suit you really!"

"Ha, ha, ha! Nora, you are too funny. But never mind; tell me what you really do think about these two rascals."

"It is as I say. I am morally sure of it. They have come to Arran thinking they would be sure to find us here, *somewhere* on the island. Probably they arrived last night only. Corrie is the first place the steamers call at, at least those that come from Greenock. They probably intend to waylay us there, or at Brodick or at Lamlash, — and I daresay the wretches will telegraph to Whiting Bay and Loch Ranza for information as to any yacht that may have put in?"

"I don't suppose they can know the name of our yacht?"

"Harry might have — no, I am *sure* he would n't be so mean! Oh no, I don't suppose they know."

"And neither saw you at the inn?"

"Dear, have you forgotten Wilfrid's appetite? Poor dear Dick was *rather* melancholy, I thought. I daresay it was only because the marmalade was a new and inferior brand."

" But would not the landlady tell them of the lady who so abruptly left the inn the moment she set eyes on the gentlemen, — and this after having ordered breakfast?"

Leonora bit her lip perplexedly. It was annoying, but probable.

" They will learn all, I doubt not," she answered coldly. " But we have the start of them."

" They have *steamers*, Nora."

" *Whew!* I forgot that. Never mind, we'll study the map and the steam-routes, and evade them yet. I know this much, that no steamers sail from Arran to Loch Fyne."

At that moment, a pistol-shot re-echoed from Corrie. At the end of an umbrella a napkin waved.

CHAPTER XVI

THE excitement on the *Belle Aurore* was intense. Some inkling of the truth had gone from mouth to mouth. Repetition had brought certainty.

Would the ladies surrender? If so, what would happen? Would the voyage come to an end? Would the wages be duly paid? Would Mr. Wester and Mr. Adair take command? Would they want a male crew? Would they — and so on — and so on.

Above all, the question of the moment was: Would they surrender? Miss Macfee thought they would. Murmuring "Whom God hath joined together let no man put asunder," she added; "They'll give in, but they'll pretend they're gaun ashore to look for a preemrose or to speer at some body or other whaur this or that auld ruin is. I ken them weel, thae fine leddies."

"Faith, an' I 'll swear by all the Sints in Hiven that they 'll do nothing so demeanin' to ladies o' quality. Bless the dear hearts av thim, they 'll give their husbands the go-by, — an' good luck to thim, says I, for all the Presbyterian Bibles in the worrld, wid all respecs to *you*, Miss Macfee!"

"Forward, there!" cried Mrs. Wester, at this moment, "where 's that girl Polly?"

"Here, mum, here she is! Go aft, you scallywag!"

"Polly!"

"Yes 'm!"

"Go down to the cabin and bring me the glass."

Captain Wester spoke in a cold, uninterested tone. The crew burned.

When Polly bolted on deck with the telescope, Leonora took it, and calmly rubbed the smaller lens while she maintained a casual conversation with Honor.

"Be Jasus, she 's a cool wan she is!" muttered O'Leary, admiringly.

At last, Captain Wester brought the glass to her right eye. She stared fixedly at Corrie.

Every one on the *Belle Aurore*, from Captain Adair to Polly, strained their ears to hear what would follow.

" It is a man.   A waiter, I presume."

" We can see it 's a man, dear, but why a waiter," interjected Honor, impatiently.

" It is a napkin that he is waving.   What sane person would run about the rocks waving a napkin, except a waiter? "

" But the pistol-shot? "

" Ah, yes, the pistol-shot ; I think that must have been by order of the landlady. It was probably a reminder that we are expected to pay for the breakfast I ordered. It is doubtless a custom in these parts." Honor stifled a laugh.   It would not do to laugh, with that delighted expression, in the eyes of the crew.

" But — eh — ah — who is he — that is, what does he want — waving that absurd napkin at the end of his umbrella.   Waiters don't carry umbrellas as well as napkins."

" It maybe an Arran habit.   But in any case, I do not know the man."

It was conclusive.   That voice could not prevaricate.   It was icily cold and indifferent.

For form's sake, and noting the impression that Leonora's audacious misstatement had made, Honor repeated, —

" You do not know the man, you say? "

" Certainly not."

A second pistol-shot re-echoed. A convulsive start showed that the *Belle Aurore's* nerves were ajar.

" Mrs. Moriarty ! "

" Yes 'm."

" Keep the yacht's course well to the nor-westward, and as close to the shore as may be safe. We want to see the scenery of this part of Arran, and *may* take a look in at Loch Ranza, though that 's rather out of our way. And now, Honor, suppose we go below and have breakfast."

The moment they had gone Miss Macfee remarked, with mingled bitterness and triumph : —

" It 'll be them fine gentry frae the *Sea-Hawk*. It 's extraordinar' what folk 'll dae just for the sake o' deein' what 's forbidden."

But Mrs. Moriarty had seized the glass. After a prolonged stare, she put it down, and went forward, a look on her face of a beaming joy.

"It's thim — it's *thim !* It's the 'usbans !"

"Indade now — well, well, for sure, an' is that so?"

"It is, Bridget O'Leary, an' God be praised for that same. How do I know? H'ant I seen the face av ould Wester — not that he's so ould either, or so bad lookin' too when it comes to that — in the cabin o' his lady? An' I'm a lost soul for iver an' a day, if that ain't Wester 'imself gallyvantin' about on thim rocks, with an umbrelly in the two hands av him an' a good ould hotel napkin — wid a hole in it, I can see — wavin' at the wrong end o't."

"An' the shot, Mrs. Moriarty? Who fired that? Was he for shootin' av us an' his lady?"

"It was his friend. He's at it agin — God kape his soul onaisy for this when he gets to Purgatory !"

Whisp — whap — crack !

The third signal was just audible. A hearty laugh of relief went up from all.

"Faith now, if we'd only a gun on board

we cud give them a good-by in the same
coin ! Well, well, I must be off an' see to
that second supply o' iggs an' bacon the
Captings — the blessin' av God be on thim
— will be hollerin' for in a minute or two ! "

In a few minutes the yacht was racing
across Sannox Bay, with Honor and Leonora
each at a port-hole — the breakfast temporarily deserted — because of the glory of
the view. To their left the conical mountain
known as the Cioch na h' Oighe rose up
clothed with the beauty of the morning light,
and still glistening with dew. Further inland, the hills known as Fergus' Seat, The
Witch's Step, and the Peaks of the Castles,
reared their serrated crests. From the
heights above Glen Sannox was audible, even
above the surge of the sea, as the yacht raced
along, the song of the innumerable small
waterfalls and cataracts on the mountain-
slopes. Behind and above the dark forms
arched a sky of glorious blue, just flecked
here and there with a snow-white cloudlet.

By the time breakfast was over, the yacht,
leaning well over as she slipped along like a
greyhound, drove past the gigantic débris

locally called the Fallen Rocks. Thence, instead of keeping by the Cock of Arran and so round into the Sound of Kilbrennan so as to make for Loch Ranza, as originally arranged, its course was made across the wide sea-stretch of the Sound of Bute, on a free tack for the Isle of Inchmarnock.

Hence, in less than half an hour, those on board got another lovely view, past Ardlamont Point and up the Kyles of Bute, to where Ben Bhreac and Ben Capnill rose above Tighnabruaich, and the Kyles seemed to merge into a landlocked narrow loch, amid a wilderness of hills.

It was exciting to tack and retack in this fresh and beautiful morning, with an ideal yachting wind to " play " with. Never had Honor and Leonora enjoyed anything like it, and their spirits rose to ecstasy-point.

Then, too, was there not the excitement of pursuit? Perhaps at that moment Richard and Wilfrid were maturing a scheme which would result in speedy capture !

" Honor ! " exclaimed Leonora, with a gesture of mock despair.

" What is it now, Nora? Not a gunboat

bearing down upon us, with the offended Majesty of the Law on board, and Mrs. Grundy with chains for our incarceration in her properly conducted respectable Domestic Mansion?"

"No. Tell me: do you think Dick and Wilfrid are quite such donkeys as — ah — they look?"

"I'm not sure, dear. Men are so deceptive. They find it easy to put on an air of sapience. I think it comes from smoking, and their habit of carrying their money loose so that they can feel it. As for Wilf and Dick, I don't think they are *idiots*, you know!"

"Do you fancy they — or one of them — would have the gumption to think of *one* thing to do, that *we* should think of were we pursuing."

"What is that? To telegraph for a balloon?"

"No — but — well, upon my soul, as Dick says, that's a notion! Really, it would be a splendid thing to do. If ever they pay us back by going off on a yachting cruise, we'll try that plan! Imagine their astonishment if they found themselves

' shadowed ' by a balloon, with their deserted wives fixedly regarding them from
aloft, and every now and again reminding
the dear men of their spouses by dropping
some little missile, say a few eggs, or a bar-
relful of flour ! It would be splendid ! "

" It is too good ever to be true, Nora,
darling ! But now, what is your idea ? "

" Well, if I were Richard, I should telegraph to Rothesay, over there in Bute, and a
great boating place, for a small steam-yacht
or steam-pinnace. In that guide-book in the
cabin, it says, yachts and small screw-steam-
ers of all sizes, can be hired in Rothesay by
the day, week, or month. They could have
one sent to them within an hour after their
telegram. If so, they could catch us up
before sundown, as easily as — as — we 've
escaped from the *Sea Hawk !* "

" Not at the rate we 're going at just now."

" You forget we have to tack ! They
would sail a straight course. It would be a
case of a weasel and a rabbit in an open
field. We should be the rabbit."

" Then what are we to do ? "

" Escape."

" Yes, but how? "

" In the first place, I doubt if this will occur to our dear foolish boys. But if it does, we must lead them a chase as long as is possible and then — *strategy*, and — "

" Yes, Nora, and what? "

" *Desertion*, if need be ! "

" *Desertion of the Belle Aurore ?* "

" Desertion of the *Belle Aurore*."

Honor looked at Leonora admiringly. Here was indeed an adventurer who would stick at no obstacle.

" But, dear — "

" I know. You are about to say that we cannot *swim* home, — much less take our belongings, to say nothing of the crew, with us. But what I would propose is this : If driven to the last extremity, we can surrender the *Belle Aurore* as she is, crew and all. Indeed, that would be a very pleasant turning of the tables. Dick and Wilf could n't well leave her after that, nor run her ashore. Besides, they would have to pay the crew, and the charge for the yacht and all the expenses of the cruise. In every way, Honor, it is n't a bad idea ! "

" And we ? "

" We ?   Oh, we should be all right. *We* could go off to Oban by train or coach, — if, for instance, we sail now to Strachur or Inverary, — and once there, there would be no difficulty in our getting a small screw-steamer for ourselves, — this time with a man and a boy. *We* in turn could, then, — if we and the *Belle Aurore* happened to be sailing in the same waters, — haunt our husbands ! "

" Ah, you *are* an inventive genius ! But no — let us stick to our colors as long as we possibly can. As you say, that steam-yacht or steam-pinnace idea may never occur to our good men. As likely as not, they 'll take the steamer-routes. But look here, Nora ! Just take a glance at this map. Don't you see that if we sail right up Loch Fyne we are caught in a trap ! Anywhere north of this inlet called Loch Gilp, and still more hopelessly anywhere north of the Otter Beacon, we should be caught as though we were mice and had entered the cheese-hung gate that leadeth to perdition ! "

" Yes, that is true. H'm ; they could either pursue us, and capture us somewhere in that upper thirty-mile stretch, or board us at Inverary. No, there is nothing for it but either to leave Loch Fyne alone, or else to put in at Tarbert. From there we might get away south or southeast."

" Then why stay there at all, — or at any place? We are better in the yacht."

" It was our escape I was thinking of, — I mean if Dick and Wilfrid are already after us, or will soon be after us, in a steam-yacht of some kind. Of course if we get a good start, it may be all right. Miss Macfee! — Miss Macfee! — how 's the wind for our going down the Sound of Kilbrennan?"

" Fine, mem. It couldna' be better. It 's from the nor' east, an' we 'd go down the Sound wi' this fair breeze jist as quick 's ony steamer that sails hereabouts, or verra nearly so."

" Well, put about! We 've decided to give up Loch Fyne. What's that point over yonder?"

"Skipness. It 's the beginnin' o' Cantyre, an' the first place on the Sound."

" Then down we go! Honor, did you

ever see a lovelier stretch of water? And just look, Arran is even more magnificent now than we have seen it yet. Oh, how sorry I am to leave this part, and Loch Fyne, and all these lovely lochs that we meant to visit! And then, too, it's opener sea where we're going to, and it mayn't be so pleasing for sailing! However, we can't help it; these husbands of ours, coming right after the *Sea Hawk* rovers, are the cause! We must make them pay for it, the wretches!"

No yacht had ever a finer run down the beautiful Sound of Kilbrennan. At the superb view of Loch Ranza, lying sheltered in the north-west of Arran, Honor and Leonora registered a vow of return. They had never seen anything more beautiful.

It was luncheon by the time the yacht lay off Campbeltown. Here Mrs. Wester and Mrs. Adair landed, for half an hour or so. They had telegrams to send. Their letters they cancelled.

These telegrams were to Wilfrid Adair, Esq., and to Richard Wester, Esq., at their respective hotels in London. Both were similarly worded.

" We are well and happy. Hope you are enjoying London. If we do not sail north or south we shall probably lay our course east or west. But telegrams or letters may be sent to Poste Restante, Oban, where we shall telegraph for anything to be forwarded."

The wind had now fallen considerably, and had shifted somewhat to the southeast. A weather-prophet at Campbeltown declared that it would go round to the southwest at sundown, and probably blow hard, with squally showers. This information, however, was received with equanimity; for a sou'-westerly wind would suit the *Belle Aurore* admirably on her Oban course.

As the dingey left again for the yacht, a boy strolled leisurely down to the shore.

" Mon, that's a peety," he remarked to the ancient mariner, who was gleefully fumbling the tip he had received from one of the captains.

" What's a peety? There is no mickle peety aboot leddies as know how to behave theirsels as yon folk dae !"

" It's no for that, Peter McAlpine. It's because Maister MacKechnie at the Post-

Office sent me doon here wi' guid news for the leddies, — or for wan o' them onyhow."

" Aye?"

" A telygraph cam' here not saxteen mee-nits syne. It was frae Loch Ranza, an' from a mon o' the name o' Wester, — Richard Wester. It was prepaid, an' wanted tae ken if a yat o' the name o' *Belly O'Rory* had put in here."

" Aye? an' what did Mr. MacKechnie say to that?"

" Oh, weel, he was that pleesit wi' the gab o' thae wummin yonner that he sent me aff like a gled tae catch them ap an' tell them he wad send aff an an'nswer at yince, wi' ony pertickelers."

" Aye, an' what 'll he dae noo?"

"Hoots, mon, I dinna ken, an' I dinna care."

But Mr. MacKechnie of the Post-Office was less indifferent. As soon as he learned all he could, he wired back to Loch Ranza: —

" *Yacht Belle Aurore just left bound for Oban.*"

Meanwhile the yacht sailed northward. It was no sooner round the Mull of Cantyre than a fresh breeze sprung up from the south, and good running was made, — all the more welcome as a heavy sea-swell would have made the yawl roll heavily if she had been becalmed.

The Campbeltown prophet proved a fraud, however. At sundown, the breeze fell altogether. They were now off the northeast coast of the isle of Jura, and the prospect of being becalmed thereabouts was not pleasant.

A suggestion from Mrs. Moriarty was put into effect; namely, that the yacht should be towed the two or three miles necessary to take her round the point of Jura, when she would get the benefit of any ocean-breeze there was. As long as she was in the Sound of Jura, on such a still evening, she might lie like a log.

The effort — a fatiguing one — was rewarded with success. A light but steady breeze prevailed on the open sea, blowing from the westward, a point or two southerly. The yacht answered to it beautifully, and glided along at a rate that surprised her captains and justified Mr. Macmasters's praises of her.

They kept as much to windward as practicable. Before moonrise they were nearly becalmed again, when they were to eastward of the Isles of the Sea, or Garvelloch Isles, with the big Isle of Scarba on their starboard quarter, and the small isles of the Sound of Luing on their right. But once they had crawled past the island of Belnahua, near which the yellow gleam from Fladda Lighthouse already wandered oceanward, they caught the fitful wind again and made good progress.

When off Easdale, the islet to the west of the island of Seil, they caught a vigorous breeze that had suddenly sprung up, and went racing through the Sound of Insh at a rattling speed, with every sail set and strained to the utmost. This fortunate spell lasted till they were between Minard Point in Argyll and Scanach Point in the Isle of Kerrera.

Here the calm seemed to have come to stay. Not a breath moved on the water. The moon had risen, and sent her tide of pale gold among the foamless wavelets and hollows. The extreme beauty of the scene, with the mystery of ocean southwestward, the

scattered isles to the south, the mountains of
Mull on the west, and the innumerable crags,
hills, and peaks northward and eastward on
the mainland of Argyll, made the enforced
patience a delight.

Still, it was not a place to linger in through
the night. Almost without warning, the wind
will become violent in these narrow sounds.
Moreover, in the Sound of Kerrera, at whose
further end Oban lay, there was a considera-
ble traffic of steamers and other craft, and a
constant watchfulness would have to be
held.

When within three miles of Oban the
Belle Aurore did not move an inch. The
tide would soon be on the ebb, and then,
indeed, she would actually drift back.

A loud puffing not far astern suggested an
idea to Honor. "Nora," she exclaimed
eagerly, "do you see that steam-collier?
Well, I propose we ask the skipper to take
us in tow."

"Good. By all means."

As soon as the lumpy boat was near, the
skipper was hailed. He agreed to take them
into Oban Bay for a pound, — an exorbi-

tant sum — to which Mrs. Wester cheerfully agreed, under the impression that the transaction rather redounded to her credit.

The Capital of the West Highlands looked very beautiful as they approached it, with its circle of scintillating lights, and the innumerable lamp-gleams from villas and cottages on the adjacent heights.

A large number of steamers, yachts, and divers craft were anchored or moored in the Bay, and it was not easy to find a suitable haven. At last, however, a good anchorage was got off the southeast shore.

The temptation to go ashore, late as it was, was great. But the distance to row seemed farther than it actually was, and the crew were tired after a heavy and exciting day's work.

The two friends sat for an hour or so in quiet happiness. Over their cigarettes they discussed the discomfiture of Mr. Wester and Mr. Adair, wanderers now, no doubt, up and down the Isle of Arran.

CHAPTER XVII

A T breakfast, Mrs. Wester proposed that
she and Honor should go ashore, partly
for enquiry at the Post-Office, and partly for
the sake of a good walk.

Honor was ready first. It was a delight
to walk to and fro upon the deck of the
Belle Aurore and look out upon so lovely a
view, one of the most beautiful of its kind in
the world she had heard, and could well
believe, — though the beauty of Oban can
only be seen aright in the late afternoon and
at sunset.

Having gazed over and over seaward and
bayward and inland in all directions, she
took up the glass to examine the busy main-
street of the little town, or what she could
see of it beyond the masts of the steamers,
sloops, yachts, and coal-barges along the
wharves.

Suddenly she started. Through the telescope she observed two gentlemen standing near a boat-hiring stand. They were evidently bargaining for a boat, or for a man to row them out, and one of the men pointed twice to the bay.

"Quick, Mrs. Moriarty!" she whispered. "Don't lose a moment. Up with the anchor. Set all sail you possibly can. We haven't a moment to lose. Fortunately there is a good capfull of wind coming down over the shoulder of this hill here behind us."

None of Her Majesty's crews could have managed a sudden departure with more celerity. Every one worked with a will, — Jane Lanigan and Murtagh at the windlass; Mrs. Moriarty, Miss Macfee, O'Leary, and Polly Jones, at the ropes; Captain Adair at the wheel.

Captain Wester heard the clanking of the windlass and the scraping sound of the chains as the anchor was hove up, and ran eagerly on deck.

"What's the matter, Honor?" she cried excitedly. "Can't we go ashore?"

"No. Oban is impossible."

" But why ? "

" *They* are here."

" *They* ! Not Wilfrid and Richard ! It is impossible ! "

" Look ! There on the parade, well to the left of the quay."

Mrs. Wester took the glass.

" I can see no one in the least resembling them."

" Where are you looking ? "

" Where you told me, — at the parade."

" H'm. Lower the glass a bit. You will see a boat, and in that boat a stout man rowing hard, and, in the stern of that boat, two passengers."

" Good Heavens ! You 're right ! It *is* Richard and Wilfrid ! How in the name of all that 's wonderful have they got here ? "

Honor stared disconsolately.

" But can we escape them, Honor? Is there time ? "

" We are moving quicker than they are already. If there is no hitch in clearing the bay, and if the wind holds when we get out beyond the headlands of Kerrera, we 'll soon leave them hopelessly behind."

A cheer came from forward. The jibs were now out as well as topsail and main. The froth bubbled and surged before the bows of the *Belle Aurore*. The crew had caught sight of the pursuing boat, though they had not understood they were fugitives till Mrs. Moriarty caught sight through the glass of one of the men in the stern, and recognized him as "the gintleman wi' the umbrelly an' the dish-clout."

A faint hail was heard as the yacht moved swiftly for Bhearnaig Point at the north end of Kerrera. It was unanswered.

Honor and Leonora did not look at the pursuing boat, — at least only furtively, and not through the glass.

In five minutes the yawl was close upon the Ruay Bhearnaig; in less than five minutes she would be round it and in the open sea.

"Plase your honors," cried Polly Jones, her round eyes dilated with excitement, "the gintleman 's takin' off his shirt!"

"What!"

"Ah, bedad thin, ye silly spalpeen," broke in Mrs. Moriarty indignantly, as she gave a sounding spank to Polly's ear, " an' phwat are ye annoyin' the ladies for? Shure, if they wants to go ashore, or to turn back, they can do it theirselves. No, no, indade, Mrs. Wester, mum, the gintleman's all right. He's only blowin' his nose, he is, with a big bandanna. Faith 't is a hot marnin' for rowin', an' the stout man 's about bate, I 'm thinkin'. Capting Adair, mum, jist bring her up to the wind a point or two more. We 'll be round this headland in a jiffy, an' then they may whistle. There 's wind outside, praise be to God ! "

And so it proved. A good breeze too.

The yacht now went off a point or two, and raced on a straight line nor'west, — a line that would take her past the light-house islet, at the end of the long Isle of Lismore, to starboard, and past Duart Point in Mull.

" Dip the flag three times," Leonora commanded, trying hard to keep down the exultation in her voice.

Away flew the bunting. Cheer after cheer went up from the crew.

" Ladies," said Mrs. Moriarty, addressing herself to those of the crew near her, O'Leary and Murtagh, with a sob of joy making her choke, — " Ladies, when we 're back in Cork, I 'll stand ye an eel-pie wi' Dublin Stout bekas o' this glory ! "

But the delight of the captains was dashed by fear. Steamer after steamer would soon be leaving Oban, and one or two, at least, would be bound for the long Sound of Mull. Steam-coasters, tugs, barges, wherries, — all were available. A swift yacht, too, could be hired. Even the ordinary passenger steamer for Staffa and Iona could waylay them. The steamer would not intercept them, of course ; but if Richard and Wilfrid sailed by it, they would soon pass the *Belle Aurore* and could land at Tobermory, where it would be easy to get a sailing wherry and so run the yacht to ground, so to say.

"We 're caught, I fear, Honor," whispered Leonora disconsolately : "unless we try to evade them by running up into Loch Aline, and I don't know if we can do that. The strait seems too narrow, and it may be shallow : I can't quite make out from my chart."

" What ! Salen Bay in Mull ? "

"Oh, we should be seen in a flash. No; all our chances lie in this breeze holding. Luckily those clouds look like it. We couldn't possibly have a more favorable wind for the Sound of Mull. Every other would involve our tacking to and fro."

"Well, our fate is in the hands of the gods. But we must keep a good lookout, and if the Staffa steamer, or any other for Tobermory, *should* pass us we must hug the coast of Morven as close as we can."

Fortunately, the wind was loyal. It went further, and became an eager auxiliary. Within an hour it had freshened into a stiff breeze. Tobermory was reached and passed, before the Staffa steamer came snorting along the sound. Her funnels were still belching smoke at Tobermory pier when the *Belle Aurore* drove the foam before her bows as she raced up by Ardnamurchan Point.

She was now clear. No more pursuit was possible, at least from the Staffa steamer, whose course would be southward the moment she rounded Mull.

There was one risk. If the pursuers were on the steamer, and disembarked at Tobermory, they could doubtless hire a small steam-yacht or a steam-wherry.

"Leonora Wester," cried Honor, as she turned her eyes from the dashing of the big Atlantic waves against the rocky promontory of the Cape of Storms: "there is nothing for it but the open sea!"

"I am ready, Captain!"

"You are! Then we'll hug the coast no more, and give up Skye."

"We seem to be always giving up, Honor, don't we?"

"Never mind. Skye would mean capture. Of course they'll think we've gone there, and we should be traced with fatal ease *en route*. Then, once at Skye, we are within betrayal by a score of telegraph offices. No, no, we'll put the steam-wherry out of the question anyhow."

"We'll have a toss! Even here there's a swell on, and when it blows on these waters, it can be rough with a vengeance, can't it, Mrs. Moriarty?"

"Hell for shure, an' not a wheeze short o' it!"

"Indeed!" Honor answered, with mock

politeness, " I had no idea it was so bad as that. However, we'll risk it. I don't know how *you* feel, Nora, but I *think* I've got my sea-legs now. This swell does n't make me the least bit queer, and what's more, I feel as though I don't care if it blows twice as hard, and a head wind at that!"

" Bravo, my Captain ! I don't know about the head-wind ; but here's for the open sea ! Hip, hip, hurrah !"

"Hip, hip, hurrah ! *hurrah !* Mrs. Moriarty, don't think we've lost our wits, but we've given up Skye, and we're going across the open sea. We'll make to-night for the Isle of Canna. I see in the chart that there's good anchorage even in the wildest weather, in the Strait of Sanday, between the islet of that name and Canna. So now alter the course due nor'west, — but keep us well to the windward of the Hysker Rocks, for there are heavy breakers, so the chart says, to the south of them."

" One word, if you plase, mum. For the love o' Hiven, tell me if it's chased we are, an' by *thim ?*"

" Yes, Mrs. Moriarty, we are : and by *thim.*"

"Oh, glory to God! Capting darlint, I'd sell my sowl as a potato-bucket jist for the glory av sailin' wid your honors! Oh, 't is a glad day I left Cork an' saw the swate faces av ye! An' look at Macfee when I tell her that good news: faith she'll look as sour 's a blind cat whin it licks the blackin' thinkin' it to be crame!"

"We're glad you're pleased, Mrs. Moriarty. And what's more, we think you're a brick, — and if we can give our husbands the slip it's not forgetting you we will be!"

"Ah, don't say that, Capting Adair, darlint, — an' God bless the swate Irish vice ye have, an' eyes as tantalisin' purty as Moriarty's was afore he took to drink, — no, don't be sayin' that. It's no prisint I'm wantin', only to be here at this divilry. Shure, it's a married wimmin I am mesilf, — and don't I know what it is? Holy Virgin, 't is peace on earth an' good-will to wimmen now-a-days!"

Both the captains hailed this outburst with a laugh of delight. "Honor darlint," Leonora whispered, as Mrs. Moriarty lunged forward to have the flying jib let out, "she's a treasure ! If ever we come to sea again she 'll be first officer and anything else she likes. The look of her great red beaming face is a joy in itself."

The *Belle Aurore* was now spanking through the water at a fine rate. It would have needed a swift screw-yacht to make up on the yawl as long as the wind held as it was. The exhilaration of the swirling rush through the foam-crested seas, the surge of the keen but sun-warmed wind, the glory of light in the deep blue sky, — it was delight, intoxication, madness !

Even the stern Macfee relaxed from her grim disapproval, — a dissatisfaction that had been steadily growing ever since the matrimonial desertion at Corrie.

"Guid sakes," she muttered to Jane Lanigan, her only confidant, "Guid sakes, it 's ungodly, but it 's graund ! "

No one who has ever sailed that perilous ocean-stretch between the Outer and Inner Hebrides can fail to know what heavy seas can rise, and what wild storms can sweep out of any quarter with appalling rapidity. But now, despite a rather heavy swell from the southwest, the whole vast ocean-reach was a glory of blue and gold everywhere creased with white.

Hour after hour passed by, without a break in the wind or anything more than a slight increase in the size of the waves. If all the powers and dominions of the air had declared for the *Belle Aurore* they could not have arranged more favorably. The yacht raced as though she were, as Mrs. Wester said, greased with lightning.

There was magic in that wild rush, in that sonorous surge, in that unceasing cataract of rainbow-irradiated spray which fell away from the bows. Magic, too, in the vibration of the quivering planks, in the straining of the mast and the yards, in the deep hum of the murmurous sails, in the song of the wind in the cordage, against the taut canvas, among the querulous spars.

When, at last, the sun sank to the level of the water, and for a few minutes brought the distant isles of Barra into prominence, gloriously beautiful in a glow of molten gold and crimson, the feelings of those on board could no longer be restrained.

" Be the sowl o' my gran'mother, who died at say, — an' a martyr she was to the ould man, who had a timper, the peace av God to him all the same ! — we must do something ! "

So Mrs. Moriarty : on the foredeck. The resolution was carried *nem. con.*

The first officer — and now by common consent Mrs. Moriarty had exchanged the indefinite for the definite article — at once went aft.

" Captings, the crew is bilin' ! "

" What 's that, Moriarty? " Leonora exclaimed, startled.

" Bilin', yer honor ! 'T is with blind enthusymiasm. Faith, I have n't seen the like since Tim Hoolahan married me sister Tomasina the day he came out o' Cork gaol, an' that for no harm either, the Sints forefind ! 'T was only a black eye he 'd given to a constable on his way to the station, an' him no more than *warm* wid the comfort av a dhrop."

" A shame ! Moriarty ! a shame ! And a man like Tim Hoolahan too ! "

" Did ye know him, Capting? " broke in the first officer eagerly.

"Well, no. But he must have been a fine man to have been worthy of Tomasina, if Tomasina was the least like *you*."

"Shure now, darlint, 't is a good lick at the Blarney Stone ye 've had! O Capting Wester, mum, an me so innycint!"

"Moriarty, when I 'm a saint in heaven, I 'll ask nothing better than to have a seat near *you*. You would amuse — eh — ah — let us say the redeemed and perfected Macfee."

Mrs. Moriarty dropped her voice here, and in mysterious tones whispered : —

"Indade, mum, 't is thinkin' a kettleful too much o' Hiven she is night an' day jist now. — an' by the same token she 's been at the Bible agin an' agin an' had tay three times this blessed day wid no meals goin', an' iver since that — that umbrelly — that umbrelly waved that ould napkin about, wid a hole in it, — as I says to her at the toime, an' she glum as a poker in a fire wid the fire out, — wid a rint in it dishgracin' to a dacint inn, let alone the man wid the umbrelly bein' a gintleman, an' God knows if—'

"Stop! Stop! You 're off, Moriarty! A

railway train's nothing to you. And you're all mixt up, — the inn and the gintleman and the hole and the napkin and tay at the wrong time, and the Bible and Macfee, to say nothing of the Almighty!"

"Och, shure, an no harm mint! Well, well, Capting Adair, mum, what I comed aft for to say is this. The sun's jist drippin' into the say — an' there's not a boat in sight astern — an' we slippin' along like rum out o' a bottle on a Saturday noight! — an' we thought it ud be a good thing, bekas o' the thankfulness we have, barrin' Macfee, that we showed it by the laste bit o' a confligration."

"By a conflagration, Mrs. Moriarty? That would be rather dangerous, would it not?"

"Oh, ye don't take my maynin', mum. 'T is a little blow-up, I mane. If ye had a gun, now! or even a fowlin' piece — or for the matter o' that a pistol — the noise we cud make wid it ud wake the dead in the deep say!"

"Alas, we haven't. But couldn't you fill the kettle with gunpowder and blow up the cuddy?"

" Ah, 't is laffin' at me, ye are, Capting ! "

" No, indeed. I would n't think of such a thing. But let us dip the flag three times and give a rousing cheer. It 's safe enough. There 's no one to hear us out hereabouts."

And what cheers they were ! And what a dipping that ensign got !

And then — the dinner !

The dishes triddled about now and again ; the planks groaned and creaked ; there was a frequent roll and an occasional plunge ; but Honor and Leonora both laughed gleefully.

The sea-fiend was laid.

If once he thought he had slipped in to spoil that joyous feast, he paid bitterly for his presumption, — for he fell into the Monopole *extra sec*, and was drowned in that frothed and sparkling liquid gold. If his wan corpse had any life left in it when the bottle was emptied, as it was with an expedition that would have made Richard P. — connoisseur as he was — proud of his wife and her friend, its last convulsion would have quiveringly died out when the cigar-ettes were lit.

Wives in Exile

O happy audacity! Brave heroism of women, ever more dauntless than poets and other timid gentles would have them! A dinner, wrought marvellously by Moriarty, with champagne and *parfait amour* and black coffee, with cigarettes as the incense after the festival, — and all this in a roughish sea out on the stormiest part of the stormy Hebridean seas!

Was it the excitement of that wonderful day — or the champagne — or the *parfait amour* — that sustained them even when, at moonrise, they went on deck and found the *Belle Aurore* with half her sail taken in, and the mainsail with what Leonora called a couple of tucks in it, and all around them a dark sea filled with leaping white waves?

Not a qualm seized them, and, when at last they turned in, they undressed with light hearts, and at once fell into slumber so deep that, hours later, they did not hear the clanging rush of the anchor as the yacht nosed wind and tide in Canna haven.

283

"SO, we're in Canna, Miss Macfee?" remarked Honor, pleasantly, to that officer when she came with a cup of tea at seven bells.

"Aye, mem, we are; an like to bide here for a spell inta the bargain."

"Oh, why's that?"

"The weather's gaun into a gale, wi' floods of rain. Canna ye hear it?"

"Yes, I *do* hear both the rain and the wind. But the yacht is as quiet as a mouse, — except for a slight swell."

"It's God's providence, mem, we are whaur we are. If we war oot on the open sea the noo, we'd hae the watter aboon our ears I'm thinkin'. We're just tuckit awa' as snug an' safe as though we war in a dry dock. We're in Castle Bay, in the hollow o' Sanday, an' sheltered from every wind

that can blaw, an' maist o' all from this wild
westerly gale that 's makin' siccan a weary
warstle oot yonner on the open sea."

"There 's no saying how long we may be
here, then?"

"Nane ava. We maun bide till the win'
gaes doon, — an' by the look o't there 's mair
to come."

"Have the crew got oilskins and sou'-
westers?"

"Aye, mem, they have that."

"Well, just go and see that they have hot
coffee or tea whenever they want it, and if
you think it advisable for them to take something stronger, well let them have it."

With that Miss Macfee went, and left the
two captains chatting cosily from their bunks.

"Is n't this luxury, Nora?" Captain Adair
exclaimed, tucking the blankets about her,
"to hear the wild wind and rain outside,
and to lie here and not need to care a straw
about it! Why, there is n't even a drag at
the anchor."

"And to know, too, that we are safe from
pursuit! They would never look for us here;
and in any case this gale will prevent any

boat, whether sailing vessel or steamer, making for Canna to-day."

And a pleasant restful day it proved, though there was little fresh air to be had because of the drenching rain, and nothing to be seen on account of the sea-mist.

It was delightful, however, to lounge about in that pleasant cabin, and read or chat or idle, just as the spirit moved one to do. Mrs. Wester, indeed, declared that she had never before known that it was possible to read in summer with the same gusto as in wild winter weather.

By the evening, nevertheless, they had begun to weary a little. The ceaseless sough of the wind was depressing, and the rain came down as though the sea of the antipodes had made a somersault and were pouring upon these northern waters.

By eight bells in the first watch there was no change. Honor and Leonora decided that bed was the best place wherein to sulk, and they did so so successfully that each forgot all about the other and sank into a happy sleep.

Next morning they had the welcome news

that the rain had stopped at last, and that the gale had moderated slightly, though still a stiff one.

They had made up their minds to another day's enforced idleness; but a surprise awaited them.

About noon a small boat put off from the Canna shore, and soon was alongside.

"There will pe nobody at all at all at the Castle," explained the very Highland boatman, a shock-headed, red-haired, freckled young man, tall and bonily angular; "an' there's need for ta help at ta ither end o' the island. A yacht will pe going ashore there."

"*Will* be going?" repeated Mrs. Wester, "but why cannot it be warned off in time?"

"Hoots, leddy, it will pe going, I am for tellin' ye, an' it is no longer any time for it to have gone to nor'ard or suth'ard."

"And what's happened?" asked Honor, who understood the predicament.

"Oh, she's just gone to pieces, she has."

"No lives lost, I hope?" Mrs. Adair broke in, eagerly.

"Na, na, sure an' there are no lives that

will pe dying; only the yacht she will pe all in pieces, an' the shentleman that sails her he is for lyin' down wid ta sorrow for that he cannot pe upon Greenock when he wants."

"We must see to this castaway, Nora. Let us go at once. Our friend here will take us."

The rumor proved to be true. On the west side of Canna a yacht had been driven on to the rocks and had foundered, fortunately not till after the small crew of two men and a boy had got safely ashore, as well as the owner.

The latter came to meet the ladies.

He was a tall, good-looking man, with the unmistakable bearing of distinction. His short grayish hair fitted close to his bronzed face, with its clean-cut features, dark moustache, and keen gray-blue eyes. In a few words he explained his disaster; how he had left Loch Maddy in South Uist, despite the weather warnings of the wise fishermen, but determined to get to Greenock as soon as he could; that is, in his yacht. The *Foam*, however, was caught in the central swing of the gale, and despite all that could be done to avert the disaster, was driven to destruction against Canna.

He was an Englishman; that was evident from his voice and accent. Soon they learned from him who he was: Sir Jasper Wingrave, of Llanidloe Hall, in West Hereford.

Honor and Leonora introduced themselves, and explained as much as they saw fit. Then, learning that there was no inn on Canna, and that the factor was away and his house shut up, and that the Castle was not yet opened for the summer, they offered him the accommodation of the *Belle Aurore*.

"We have a spare cabin, Sir Jasper," Mrs. Wester added cordially, "and you are welcome to it, and to such hospitality as we can give you, till this gale abates, which will probably be to-morrow."

"Alas, dear lady, it is much more likely to spring up anew. I know these seas well. But even if it does n't I can't expect to get away from here for a week at least, — for there's no south-steamer due for six days yet, and there does n't seem to be a smack, coble, or wherry in the island at present. Would nothing tempt you — wind and weather permitting — to take me across to Sligachan in Skye, or to Arasaig in Argyll, or to Tobermory in Mull?"

"Well," Leonora began hesitatingly, " we are eagerly awaiting a chance to get on to the Hebrides, and every hour is of importance to us. Still, of course, if — if — of course, if you *cannot* get away by any other means, we'll put the *Belle Aurore* back. Only, not at Tobermory. If all the same to you, Sligachan in Skye would be the best for us."

"Sligachan be it, madam. And you have me your grateful debtor for evermore. I thank you both heartily for your great courtesy. And now, as I am rather wet and chill, and as you have filled me with curiosity to see the *Belle Aurore*, I throw myself on your mercy straightway."

"And your men, Sir Jasper?"

" They are arranged for, Mrs. Adair. They will stay here till the steamer comes six days hence. Fortunately both are Gaelic islemen, so they will be quite happy here ; and as for the boy it will be a delightful spree for him."

"Then come ! We cannot offer you a

change of clothes, — though you said, I think, that most of your wardrobe had been got out before the *Foam* went down? — but we can promise you a good dinner, good wine, and good coffee."

"And what is best of all, — though you do not need to promise it! — good company. A little while ago I was sorry for the loss of the *Foam;* now I rejoice at it."

CHAPTER XIX

SIR JASPER was right. The gale increased towards evening, after a temporary lull, and the rain came down as though its previous efforts were a mere shower or two.

Nevertheless a delightful evening was spent on the *Belle Aurore*. Sir Jasper Wingrave was a man who knew how to rise to an occasion, and an occasion such as that which had just happened might not occur to him again in eternity.

He was charmed with everything; with his hosts most of all, with the dainty dinner provided by Mrs. Moriarty, with that lady herself, with the crew, with the whole escapade. Fervently he prayed that no steamer would put in at Canna. His fear was a search-boat of some kind; for the gale had been and still was so severe that great anxiety would be felt concerning all yachts at sea.

As for Honor and Leonora, they were well content, for Sir Jasper was one of the most amusing and delightful companions they had ever met. A cosmopolitan, he seemed to have sojourned in every country, to have friends in every land, and to see the good side of every nation. They could read between the lines, and see that he had served with distinction, both as a political officer and as a diplomatist.

There was only one thing that disturbed them. What would Richard and Wilfrid think about the *Belle Aurore* ? If they had any reason to believe that the yacht had not gone to Skye, or kept to the haven-frequented coast, they would be terribly anxious about her fate. The storm had been far more violent than they had surmised. In their safe " burrow," as Sir Jasper laughingly called it, they could hear the wild surge of the wind and the roar of the sea, but even thus had been unable to realize that the gale was, as this castaway assured them, one of the worst that had swept those seas for a long time.

Nor could he hold out much hope of fine weather. After the too fine spring, he said, there was bound to be a stormy summer, and, apologizing for being so ill conditioned a prophet, he foretold gale after gale till the Clerk of the Weather had got over his sulks.

All this brought about a decision on the part of the captains of the *Belle Aurore.*

That night, before they turned in, and after they had discussed Sir Jasper thoroughly, they agreed that they would set sail for the Frith of Clyde the moment they could venture to do so. At Greenock they would be sure to find definite word as to the whereabouts of their bewildered spouses, and could communicate with them. Then, too, it would be safer and pleasanter to voyage about among the beautiful lochs that reach from the Frith in all directions.

Honor did not tell Leonora, nor did Leonora hint to Honor, that the prolonged company of Sir Jasper Wingrave was a further inducement.

Next morning that gentleman learned, by a chance allusion he made, that his friends Colonel Lascelles and the Master of Ruthven were yachting in the West of Scotland.

For a moment the ladies were embarrassed.

"Have you seen them recently," their guest asked, with his eyes concentrated on the interior of the egg he was eating, for in a glance he had noted that the mention of the names had brought a flush to the faces of his companions.

"Yes," Mrs. Wester replied, with rather too emphasized nonchalance, "we saw them a short time ago. They were, I think, going to sail to Greenock. Their yachting trip was about over, and they had to give up the *Sea Hawk*."

"The *Sea Hawk*? That is not the name of Lascelles' boat. What was it, — a screw or a sailing yacht? A yacht? — oh, then, there must be some mistake. He has a fine screw-yacht, the *North Star*, a boat of about a hundred tons. If he were in the *Sea Hawk* it must have been for a short cruise while he was waiting for the *Star*. What a pleasant fellow he is!"

"Very."

"And Douglas Stuart, too?"

"Yes, charming."

"Where did you meet them? You were old acquaintances, I suppose?"

"Oh, we met them off the Lamlash side of Arran. Mrs. Adair and I were away from the *Belle Aurore* on a brief excursion. We met."

"Ah, I see."

But a little later, Honor betrayed the mystery. He was delighted; and privately thanked his stars that fortune had behaved more kindly to him.

The rest of the day passed pleasantly. Both captains declared that they did not mind how long the bad weather lasted. In the heart of each, however, there was a slight qualm. Was not Sir Jasper Wingrave *too* delightful a companion? And — and — whom did he really prefer, — Honor or Leonora? A faint odor of heart-burning began to blend with the fragrance of blithe happiness which prevailed.

That evening, Miss Macfee gave notice.

"But why, Miss Macfee?" expostulated Mrs. Wester, while Honor sat by with a quiet smile.

"Weel, mem, to be frank, I'm not carin' for what's goin' on."

"What do you mean, Macfee?"

"We're no sailin' onywhaur, an' — an' — ye ken weel yer husbands maun be gae ankshious aboot ye — an' — an' — what wi' this an' what wi' that — I jist think I maun ask tae be excused frae further service as soon as ye git to a place whaur I can leave ye'."

"As you like, Macfee. You will have an opportunity soon ; for if the weather permits we think of leaving to-morrow for Greenock, which Sir Jasper is anxious to reach as soon as he can, and where we hope to hear of Mr. Adair and Mr. Wester."

This politic answer wrought a complete change in Miss Macfee. Her primness thawed, and for the rest of the evening she was almost officiously agreeable. When she came to Mrs. Wester's cabin, when the lights were put out, and heard that the captain had decided to make for Greenock, she withdrew her resignation.

"Then don't be such a fool again, Miss Macfee."

"Indeed, mem, I winna. But I've not been weel, partly wi' this weather, — sic weather as nae mortal body could expec' at this time o' the year — an' partly wi' Mrs.

Moriarty, who has the morals o' a cat an' the manners o' a scallywag, tho' the Lord kens what that means, tho' she 's aye usin' it."

And it was the repentant Macfec herself who, an hour after sunrise, came with the good news that, though the skies were still gray and lowering, the wind had fallen to a pleasant breeze, and that the sea had moderated considerably.

With Sir Jasper's willing help, the *Belle Aurore* was soon under weigh. He took the wheel, for careful steering would be necessary the moment the yacht emerged from the calm strait into the still turbulent open sea.

Honor and Leonora took but a slight interest in breakfast; in fact, so interested were they in some books they had that they did not rise from their bunks till late in the afternoon.

By this time the yacht was well south. The morning breeze had freshened into a strong wind from the north, and so the utmost possible running was made.

Sir Jasper politely consulted with Mrs. Moriarty, and they agreed to sail due south.

The captains, however, were temporarily

subdued, not beaten. As the yacht passed
a mile or two to the westward of Iona, they
came on deck to get a glimpse of the famous
island, where it lay low in the sea against
the wonderful background of the Mull
Mountains.

From that time onward, too, they acted
as skippers. Not even a suggestion was
allowed to be made by the guest, who was
reminded that he was only a castaway and
must be obedient. He gladly obeyed.

The sun set luridly as they sighted the
Mull of Cantyre, and by the look of the wild
sky to westward, though it boded fresh wind
rather than wet, they were glad to know that
the bow of the *Belle Aurore* would in an
hour or two be pointing northeastward.

A fitful moonlit evening, with driving
clouds and occasional scurries of rain, followed; and by the time the Mull was
actually rounded, a heavy fall again began.
The wind, too, slackened under the lee of
the Cantyre coast.

When Mrs. Wester and Mrs. Adair woke
next morning, it was to find the yacht slowly
gliding northward off the south coast of

Arran, and within sight of the spot where they had so nearly ended their voyage in tragic fashion.

Sir Jasper assured them that the wind would certainly freshen the moment it veered a little more to the southwest, as it was trying to do; and shortly after luncheon his prophecy was fulfilled.

In a spanking sou'west breeze the yacht raced up the Frith, taking the course between Garroch Head at the mouth of Bute and the two Cumbraes. An hour later they were off Wemyss Bay, and in the beautiful reach between the west coast of Renfrewshire and the lovely east coast of the Cowal, clothed with wood and studded with villas and cottages almost in an unbroken line from Toward Point to Dunoon.

But not even the beauty of the scene could raise the spirits of Honor and Leonora.

What was the reason? Alas, they put their despondency down to every cause but the right one.

Sir Jasper Wingrave would have to bid farewell to them in an hour or so. To each, there came with this thought a sentimental regret that was allowed to wear a richer apparel.

"But," thought Honor, "it is possible after all that he cares for Leonora more than he does for me." (Then, aloud to her colleague : —)

"I wonder what he will do, Nora, what he will think when he leaves us? How strange it is that a man like that never married! By the way, I think we've rather taken it for granted that he is a bachelor."

"Oh, no, I am sure he is unmarried. There is a look about him as though he were so happy and contented — and —" .

"Oh, Nora! Nora! — *Hist*, here he comes."

In less than an hour the *Belle Aurore* lay off Greenock at the Tail of the bank.

On Prince's Pier they could plainly see some one waving. Was it to them?

How were they to know that the Laird of Canna, who had been fishing in the South Hebrides, had returned to the island an hour or so after they had left it ; had heard of the wreck of the *Foam*, and of the safety of his friend Sir Jasper Wingrave ; of the safety, also, of the yacht, *Belle Aurore*; and of the departure of the latter for Greenock, with Sir Jasper on board.

"Who can it be?"

"I think I can guess, Mrs. Wester," Sir Jasper answered, with an inscrutable smile.

"It is, I fancy, Lady Wingrave."

"Lady Wingrave?"

"Yes. My wife."

Honor and Leonora looked at each other. After all, their eyes seemed to say, yachting *à deux* was tiresome. Had they not better wire for Richard and Wilfrid?

"You must let me go ashore and bring my wife back to thank you for all your kind and generous care of me."

"We shall be delighted, Sir Jasper," Honor answered, her voice cordial, her eyes grave.

It did not take long to write *Finis* to this brief episode. During Sir Jasper's absence Honor and Leonora made no remarks. Each wondered why the other did n't speak, or go below, or do something.

When the dingey came out again, ten minutes later, Sir Jasper stepped on board,

and helped up a pleasant-eyed and distin-
guished-looking woman of about five and
thirty, — beautiful, Honor thought, though
Mrs. Wester admired the type more than the
individual, perhaps because she was of the
same type as Honor, and there could be no
rival to that dear and beautiful comrade.

Tea and chit-chat passed the time pleasantly enough, but it was a relief to all when
Lady Wingrave rose and said that she must
go.

As for their late guest, both Honor and
Leonora discerned in him a certain uneasi-
ness : was it mourning, or quiet amusement?

In either case, it was now well to — set
sail !

They would be off again at once, they said,
as they declined the Wingraves' invitation to
dine with them, — but would Sir Jasper call
at the Post-Office and send them on any
letters or telegrams addressed to them, to the
Poste Restante, Dunoon?

And so — *explicit.* The episode was
taken hold of by the indifferent hand of
Time, docketed, and marked " *Over.*"

" Mrs. Moriarty," Leonora remarked

quietly, " I am glad you have kept the sails on. Let her pay off, we are not going to stay here to-night."

It was a disappointment, but there was solace for the first officer in the knowledge that Miss Macfee would fume and fret.

" Where to, Capting Wester? "

" Oh, go down by the Cloch Lighthouse again. Then tack across the Frith and bring us up for the night in Dunoon Bay."

But the day was not to end in dull reaction.

As the *Belle Aurore* glided southward, a yell from Mrs. Moriarty startled Honor and Leonora out of their despondency.

" What on earth 's the matter with Moriarty? " exclaimed Mrs. Wester, as she stared with astonishment at that officer, who stood with her right arm rigid, and apparently pointing at the Lighthouse as though it were a ghost.

" What is it, Moriarty? "

But Honor had already seen, and understood.

There was the *Sea Hawk*, not quarter of a mile away, and coming straight towards them !

"Out with every stitch of sail you can," she cried. "Up with the helm! Let her go, Mrs. Moriarty."

All was now wild bustle and temporary confusion. Honor herself gave a hand, while Leonora took the wheel.

The yacht came hard up to starboard, payed off and raced away on a northeast tack, her bowsprit facing Strone Point where it divides the Holy Loch from Loch Long.

They could clearly discern two men standing aft on the *Sea Hawk* shouting and waving frantically.

"So much for the manners of Colonel Lascelles and Mr. Douglas Stuart," said Honor, indignantly.

"Impudent wretches," Leonora added. "And Honor! don't let us look at them! If we take up the glass, they'll see us doing it. Let us ignore them altogether."

"Yes; but ignoring won't do much good. We're on the wrong tack to escape them. We must either go up Loch Long or into the Holy Loch as we're bound, — and then they'll have us in a trap."

"Then round with us at once, and let us

race them. I'm *sure* the *Belle Aurore*'s much the better boat."

So once more the yacht swung round, and now went flying down the Frith with her bow towards Inellan.

The *Sea Hawk* got her spanker out, and followed with the foam sweeping from her bows.

Suddenly Mrs. Moriarty began a chuckling laugh.

"What is it, Captings dear? It's well; askin' that ye may be. In the first place 't is gainin' we are, an' at ivery yard. In the nixt place, look at that yonder!"

"What's *that?*"

"Why, Capting, it's mist — fog — sea-fog; that's what it is, the Sints be praised. We'll be in it in tin minnuts, an' then the *Sea Hawk* may dance till her bowsprit nips her helm, an' she won't find us, save by a fhluke, which God forefind!"

Probably those on the *Sea Hawk* noted both these points. The waving still continued, and the flags flew in some signal which nobody on board the *Belle Aurore* could interpret, or would have cared to do if they could.

At last a gun was fired.

The captains smiled.

"They may blow up, if they like," said Leonora, calmly, "but we won't pay the least attention."

But Mrs. Moriarty's prophecy was more than fulfilled, for in half the time she had specified they were right into a bank of driving sea-mist.

The moment they were well enshrouded, the course was altered somewhat; and the yacht went off upon the larboard tack, hard for the Cumbraes.

"We'll go round Bute and past Arran, and get safe into Tarbert, Honor, after all !"

"Hurrah ! *Addio*, Colonel Lascelles ! *Addio*, Mr. Douglas Stuart ! "

CHAPTER XX

AND in due time Tarbert was reached. The morrow proved a wet and stormy day, and Honor and Leonora contented themselves on board.

That evening, however, they went ashore. naturally they inquired at the Post-Office for any letters or telegrams. There were no letters, but four telegrams were handed to them, two to each.

These duplicates, each signed by the respective husbands, ran as follows : —

(1) (Dated five days earlier) : "*If this reach you, wire at once, c/o Dundonald, Boat Builder, Greenock.*"

(2) (Bearing the current date) : "*Await us in Tarbert if you call there, we expect to arrive there this evening.*"

Here was an awkward predicament. Mrs. Wester and Mrs. Adair at once turned. At the pier they learned that the second steamer

308

was due about seven. Unfortunately, no other steamer called, either northward or southward bound, till the morrow. Still more unfortunately a calm prevailed, and the little wind there was blew straight for Tarbert Harbor. It was now just turned six; there was no time to get the yacht out of the harbor, or to sail her out of the sight of the incoming steamer.

"Caught at last, Honor!" Mrs. Wester exclaimed with half angry, half amused despair.

"No, not *quite* yet, Nora. I have a plan. Here it is. You know that this is an isthmus? Well, a mile or less from here, the narrow West Loch Tarbert runs straight to the Atlantic. Down this West Loch Tarbert a steamer for the Island of Islay runs. Three days a week at this season there is an extra evening run, on the arrival of the *Iona* here. A trap waits at this pier to take passengers across, — there it is, yonder! Carriages, also, — there *they* are!"

"Well?"

"Well, my plan is this: We go on board now, and arrange with Mrs. Moriarty. She must say that the birds are flown; and that her instructions are to wait here till she hears from wherever we go to (that is, *don't* go to), and that although we may not return for a month to come."

" Yes, and what then?"

"Then we must take a few necessaries with us, and go ashore again. We shall hire the foremost of those carriages, and seat ourselves. From there we can have an uninterrupted view of the passengers who land at this pier. If we see Richard and Wilfrid, we can at once decamp. They will, of course, have descried the *Belle Aurore*. While they are boarding us, we'll be on board of the West Loch Tarbert boat, and on our way to Islay!"

" Honor Adair, if ever a woman deserved to be called Madame Napoleon it's you! Your strategy is splendid."

All was done, accordingly. Mrs. Moriarty, somewhat saddened at being "out of it," promised to keep the secret, and also to send Polly Jones with telegraphic messages whenever advisable. By the time that the red funnels of the *Iona* appeared just outside

Loch Tarbert, the two ladies were sitting safely ensconced in a shaky but presumably drivable wagonette.

It was an exciting moment when the steamer drew alongside the pier, and the passengers began to disembark.

Two — six — ten — eleven in all! But, of Mr. Wester or of Mr. Adair, no sign!

What did it mean?

"Hae yer freens come, mem?" inquired the driver, anxiously. "Shall ye wait for them? The Islay boat doesna wait lang."

"No, there's your fare, my man. We won't go now, as the friends we were expecting have n't arrived. Or no, wait a moment! It's turned out so fine after this drizzling day that we'll go for a drive. I must just go out to that yacht there first, or rather get some one to come ashore. Ah, there goes the *Iona*. As soon as she's out of the way we'll get our dingey ashore."

The driver offered to do the summoning. He had a voice, he boasted, that would draw the nails out of a ship's keel.

As a matter of fact his wild yell of "*Moriarty* ahoy!" aroused not only that lady, and all the crew of the *Belle Aurore*, but the occupant of every fishing smack in the harbor.

In five minutes she was ashore, swiftly oared by O'Leary. The matter was discussed, and it was agreed that the ladies should call at the Hotel before they summoned the dingey to take them off.

This settled, the drive could be enjoyed; and enjoyed it was. There are few lovelier localities than the vicinage of Tarbert — when it can be seen; but it is a wet place, and only the dauntlessly sanguine take up their abode there for any length of time.

A soft velvety darkness obscured headland and bay — save where the latter was partially lit by the lanterns of the cobles and fishing smacks — when Mrs. Wester and Mrs. Adair drove back through the little town, delighted with their trip ashore after so much seafaring. They were, however, eager to get back, for a thick white mist was creeping in from the sea.

Between the last of the little shops and the Hotel at the pier they were accosted by Polly, shadowy in the sea-fog.

"Ah! Something up!" exclaimed Mrs. Wester eagerly, as she dismounted.

"Now then, Polly, what is it?"

The child spoke in an awed whisper.

"Plase, 'm! Plase, 'm! *She*'s alongside o' us."

"Why what do you mean, girl? Who's *she?*"

"The *Seok*, 'm."

"The *Scok?* What's the *Scok?*"

"O Nora!" Honor interjected, catching her breath; "she means the *Sea Hawk!*"

"Heavens! *This is* too much of a good thing. Are we *never* to be free from these people."

"Yes, 'm; and they've put a man on board in charge."

"*What!*"

"They've put a man aboard the *Belly Hooroar*, an' he's to prevent the *Belly Hooroar* goin' out; an' Miss Macfee 'as taken to a cabin she is, an' lockt herself in, an' Mrs. Moriarty 'as the high strikes an' is kickin' orful!"

"Oh, this is too intolerable, Nora, what shall we do?"

" The police are the best persons to call in, if there *are* any here.   I do declare ! To follow us like that, and actually take possession of our yacht !   Colonel Lascelles must think —"

" Oh it ain't the Kurnel, 'm, as is on the *Seok !* "

" *Not* the Colonel !   Then who is it ? "

" Plase, 'm, it's the gintleman wi' the umbrelly an' the dish-clout."

" Polly Jones, are you mad ? "

" No, 'm, plase, 'm, it ain't my fault, 'm," sniffed poor Polly, lugubriously.

" I know whom she means, Nora.   She means *Richard P. Wester !* "

" *What ?*   Oh, wait — of course — I remember now !   Polly, do you know who the gentlemen are on the *Sea Hawk ?*   Are they the gentlemen who saved us from drowning that morning off Arran? "

" No, 'm, indade, 'm, they is the gintry as was at the inn at that place you stopped at and wint ashore to see, — thim that waved an' hollered an' fired pisthols."

Honor looked at Leonora.

Leonora looked at Honor.

"What is to be done, Nora?"

"I see it all. They have chartered the *Sea Hawk*. It was *they* who pursued us after we left Greenock. And now they have tracked us, have us in a trap, and have taken possession of the *Belle Aurore*. We're done for, and must sue for pardon, and make the best terms we can."

"Not so fast, dear. I have an idea. Come here a moment."

With that, Mrs. Adair drew her friend aside. For safety's sake they had not yet dismissed the cab. They whispered their plot in the lee of that vehicle.

It was, however, no project of immediate flight. Honor scorned either retreat or capitulation.

The driver and his trap were now dismissed. The conspirators retired to the adjacent bracken-covered slope. There Honor disrobed herself of a petticoat. She and her colleague soon divided this. Then calling Polly, they went down to the beach, where the dingey lay, griding her keel in the tide-wash.

In a couple of minutes the oars were

heavily swathed in the discarded and freshly sacrificed petticoat.

"If I get my death of cold," Honor murmured, "Wilfrid must learn that it was *he* who drove me to this crucial risk!"

"Well, dear, I think we'll manage to give them the go-by after all."

"With these muffled oars and the thick mist, your plan ought to succeed."

"We'll try. 'A person too regardful of comfort never won fair Liberty,' — that's our reading, to-night, of 'faint heart never won fair lady.'"

By Honor's direction Leonora sat in the stern, with the tiller ropes in her hands; while she rowed. Polly was in the bow, face forward.

Slowly and silently the dingey crossed the little loch. When it was almost upon the rocks on the opposite side, it turned and came slowly back upon the *Belle Aurore* from the seaward side.

Unheard and invisible it glided along the starboard side of the yacht.

On the other, it would have run the risk of immediate discovery, for the *Sea Hawk* was not twenty feet away, and a casual flare of light would be. fatal.

Lightly as a feather, Polly caught the anchor-chain, scaled it, and disappeared on deck.

Three minutes thereafter the anxious, and shivering listeners could hear the heavy tread of Mrs. Moriarty, as she walked to and fro with some one of a heavier tread still. When their voices broke the stillness, there was no mistaking the unknown one for that of a man.

"Well, well, for shure, an' I'm glad you wull pe feelin' pettur, Mrs. Moriarty," Honor and Leonora heard a deep Highland voice say, with evident cordiality: and with eager ears they listened to the conversation that followed, though they lost Mrs. Moriarty's first reply.

"You are a ferry goot, ma'am, an' I'm not denyin' ut a wee drappie o' hot Caw-melton, or Talisker either for ta matter o' that, would keep awaay this ferry pat mist."

"Faith, too, an' a foine strong handsome man loike yirsilf won't be despisin' a look into a steak an' kidney pie, surrindered in bate-up potaties an' biled tommytoes?"

There was a moment's hesitation, big with fate. When the man spoke it was with a weary sigh of resignation.

"It would pe goot, ma'am, it would pe *ferry* goot, but it's not to pe leavin' the deck I am; not meanwhile whativer. An' it's a true thing it is that steak an' kidney pie is ta ferry pest food I know of."

"Mr. Macaulay, you belave me whin I tell ye that ye've niver set eyes on a pie like that which is simperin' down in the cabin jist as though it was the purty gyurl that is dyin' for yez somewhere, O you wild darin' bad man that yez are!"

A pleased Macaulayan laugh fell hoarsely out upon the mist, and then sputtered into the damp silence.

"You Irish ladies have the waay wi' you, to be shure, aye, aye, for shure! An' I a rispyectable marriet man, too, an' goin' on sixty!"

"You sixty! Faith now, Mr. Macaulay, 't is blarneying me yez are! Oh, the roguery av ye! an' me takin' ye all the toime for five an' thirty, an' not a day more, as I hope for Hivin! Ah, shure 't is manny a pore heart ye 've lid a dance ! You seafarin' min — lasteways the 'andsome rovers — are no better than the herrin' : on ye come, wid a hullabaloo, and off yez are wid a frisk o' yer tails before we poor lone wimmin can cry Jiricho ! an' see the prophet fall ! "

Again, silence. Perhaps the elderly and " rispyectable " Macaulay was pondering the unfamiliarity to his ears of Mrs. Moriarty's Scriptural allusion.

" Ah, Hivins and irth ! Am I to be forgettin' ? Why there 's rum punch too, to be had for the brewin' av it, the blessin' o' God upon it for a holy comfort to the mind above an' the belly below. An' there 's a cold ham there is, an' the lovin' breast of a duck sittin' upon green peas as though she 'ad jist layed thim ; though now I 'm thinkin' av it, it 's a young drake she was. But that steak an' kidney pie ! — Shure it 's just wasted it 'll be, clane thrown away. An' all that good whiskey, too ! Mr. Macaulay, whin it 's takin' whiskey ye are, hot, d 'ye take limmon an' sugar wid it ? "

" O really, ma'am, since it 's so ferry kind and pressin' you are for peing, an' as it 's a

night that is ferry pad for one like me, I 'm
thinkin' that if you will have one of ta girls
aft, just to keep ta decks an' a ferry goot
look-out, I will pe joining you for a look at
that pie, an' — an' — ta whiskey."

With a sigh of relief Honor whispered
to her companion that there would not be
long to wait now.

Five minutes passed ; seven ; a weary ten.
Almost upon the twelfth, a hoarse whisper
sounded above them, coming from a dark
bulk that loomed out of the mist.

"Come up, darlints ! It's bhlind drunk
he is, poor dear, an' lyin' sound as a babby
after the spasms, an' on your bed, too,
Capting Wester, darlint ! "

" Oh, the brute ! "

" Whisht ! It's as quiet as a moonbame
ye must be ! Come up this way —ah, ah,
that 's it — an' you ! ah, the Sints have their
eyes on ye ! "

Once on deck the Captains lost no time
in going below, accompanied by their invaluable first officer.

It was true. Mr. Macaulay, a sandy-
haired, sandy-bearded man of about sixty,

heavily freckled, and with a look of solemn goodness upon his face, lay on Mrs. Wester's bunk, his right hand still grasping the remains of the duck that was a drake.

"What's done it?" Leonora whispered, bewildered.

"It's this, Capting darlint."

"What, methylated spirits!"

"Yis. The Holy Virgin shoved the iday into me ould mind. I heated thim up, an' whin he 'ad his tumbler wid the whiskey in it, an' a double dose at that, I jist filled it up with thim mithylogical spirits! An' that was not wanst only! Faith, he had only put the outside av his appytite upon that pie, an' was playin' wid the duck, whin I put in the sugar, whin up he got, singin' 'Holy! Holy! Holy!' an' fell down jist as yer honours see 'm now before the blessed eyes av ye!"

"Fetch the rope, Mrs. Moriarty."

"Indade I will. Oh, 't is the peace o' God I'm havin'!"

"And you, Nora, make a gag out of this handkerchief. Polly, you run and fetch O'Leary."

In a few minutes the deed was done. Mr.

Macaulay was handcuffed, footcuffed, gagged, and ignominiously carried on deck. Thence, in turn, he was lowered into the dingey.

" Now, Bridget, you go off, and don't make a splash as you value your life. Fasten the dingey on to the *Sea Hawk*, and bring away its boat instead."

While this was being done, the anchor chain was silently payed out to the full, and then allowed to sink out of sight.

The heavy ebb that prevails on that side of Loch Fyne, and particularly off Tarbert, soon made the yacht drift from her late anchorage.

Silent as a ghost, and in a few seconds as invisible as ghosts in general, the *Belle Aurore* slid seaward. The only splash was when Bridget O'Leary, having missed the rope thrown to her on her return, made an at first unsuccessful effort to recover it.

Five minutes later the yacht was out on Loch Fyne. Slowly mainsail, foresail, and jib crawled up into the mist.

The breeze, faint but steady, filled them. A continuous froth bubbled at the bow of the yacht. Behind, a white wake slowly widened.

EPILOGUE.

. . . . . .

A week later there was a heavy gale off the north coast of Ireland.

Nowhere was it so bad as in the neighborhood of the Giant's Causeway, where the sea rose and leapt among clouds of spray.

A yacht was vainly striving to make head against a terrific drift of wind, tide, and current. Her last chance lay in her ability to weather the gaunt headland which intercepted her.

Half an hour earlier, the skipper of a steamer, passing her at railway speed, had taken a note of the name, — *The Sea Hawk.*

The doomed vessel seemed to be driving straight upon a fatal shore; for already the headland was strewn with wreckage, and a group of men and women had all the appearance of unfortunate castaways.

In this group the moving spirits were Honor Adair and Leonora Wester. They

323

did not give another thought now to their own shattered vessel, whose fragments were impaled on the reefs at their feet, or swirled to and fro in the foaming water. What did they care, now, — since they and theirs were safe, though hardly a vestige ·of the *Belle Aurore* would survive; what did they care, when the *Sea Hawk*, with their loved ones on board, seemed driving fast to a certain doom!

If the gale was bad when, two hours earlier, they had come to grief, it was much worse now. The chance of those on the *Sea Hawk* was a poor one.

Besides the disheartened and weeping crew, there were three coast-guardsmen and four fishermen of the neighborhood. All gloomily watched the approaching vessel.

"No, madam," said one of the coast-guardsmen to Honor, shouting because of the screeching of the wind, " it ud be impossible to get a boat out. The only chance for the yacht is to strike into those shallows yonder, an' then for those on board to sprawl ashore quick as lightnin' before the surge can suck them back."

"We'll save them, Nora! We'll save

them ! " cried Honor, with passionate eagerness. " I'll wave my shawl down there, and
I think they'll understand ! And then, all
of us, we must all take hands and rush in the
moment the yacht breaks up, and each of us
seize a man ! "

The brave thought inspired them, and the
signal of the shawl proved to be salvation for
those on board the *Sea Hawk*.

On she came with a wild rush.

They could see Wilfrid Adair at the wheel,
his hair flying in the wind. He had seen
Honor's signal, and understood. The yacht
was apparently leaping to her doom, like a
deer flying from wolves and springing among
crouching tigers. It seemed impossible that
she should not be transfixed and mangled
and rent into a myriad pieces upon these
awful fangs of rocks.

But an iron hand was steering, and an un-
wavering gaze fixt upon the spot where, at
imminent peril of being swept away and
drowned, Honor waved her signal.

It all happened in a few seconds. A swift
surging rush — a wild cry from those on
shore — a grinding, splitting crash —

The next moment Wilfrid Adair and Richard Wester, with their three companions had sprung into the shallows, and were reeling and struggling against the resurge.

It would have been impossible to evade death, but for the semi-circular human cordon. A cheer broke forth as one by one a castaway was rescued : soon the last had been gript, and with a sustained panting effort, all were at last dragged ashore.

If the gratitude of Honor and Leonora could be enhanced, it was because each had saved him whom she loved better than any one else in the world : but, for a time, their joy was mixt with bitter pain, for Richard Wester had been struck on the head by a piece of timber, and Wilfrid Adair had swooned, half-drowned.

But at last, speech, happiness, deep joy came to them. Over and over the married lovers kissed and hugged each other, then turned and kissed and hugged " the opposite side," as Mrs. Moriarty said.

All was forgotten in that supreme delight.

" We owe our lives to you, Honor darling," Wilfred exclaimed at last ; " and you are the bravest, sweetest, dearest wife in the world! And since no lives are lost, I'll say this, — that I'd lose a dozen yachts if only to have had the pleasure of this long chase of you, and to get you at last, — by being saved by you!"

And what a handshaking there was all round, and what happy laughter and tears, with hardly a thought for the shattered yachts, whose last fragments were already the sport of the seas.

"And who do you think is coming hard after us, Leonora?" asked Mr. Wester after a bit, when in less danger of suffocation from his wife's arms: "coming hard after us in a big steam-yacht?"

"Who?"

"Why your dear friends Colonel Lascelles and the Master of Ruthven!"

"Oh, the insolence of them! Are we never to see the last of these wretches?"

"But they saved your lives, my dear, — just as you have saved ours!"

"Oh, that is all very well: but what do they mean by following us like that?"

"Well, you know Lascelles is a famous

yachtsman, and he only had the poor *Sea Hawk* while he was waiting for his steam-yacht *The North Star.* We parted company this morning. He was to beat up the Londonderry coast, and then come after us. He 'll be here before long, I guess, for all the gale."

"So, you wretches, you hunted us in couples ! "

"Forgive us ! Never were wives so hard to catch ! "

"And so these two accomplices of yours are on the *North Star ?* "

"Yes : and they have guests that know you also, you flirtatious young parties ! Oh, yes, don't pretend you don't know. Who else than Sir Jasper Wingrave? "

"And his wife? "

"Yes, Leonora, and his wife ! "

But why go on? Of course the *North Star* came along, and safely entered the adjacent haven of Dunore, on the wind-sheltered east side of Dunore Head.

That night all the shipwrecked were to stay at the Dunore Arms. On the morrow, the crew of the late *Belle Aurore*, under the guidance of Mrs. Moriarty, were to go by train to Dublin, there to await the arrival of *The North Star*.

And what a happy company it was that sat down to dinner that night, — both in the big kitchen and in the saloon! And how deeply and often, the health was drunk of the brave and beautiful Captains of the *Belle Aurore!*

Only, while Sir Jasper Wingrave looked at his wife and thought that Lady Wingrave was Lady Wingrave forever and a day; and Wilfrid Adair looked at Honor and thought her more beautiful than ever; and Richard Wester looked at Leonora, till his heart melted, and he swore to himself he would sacrifice the hated " P " of his second baptismal name, — while *they* thought *this*, Colonel Lascelles brooded upon the Rape of an Hibernian Sabine. He had found Ideala L., the perfect Sea-Cook. And her name was Moriarty.

www.ingramcontent.com/pod-product-compliance
Lightning Source LLC
Chambersburg PA
CBHW020940030726
47496CB00005B/1275